To readers, this book would not be possible without you

CONTENTS

1

"What happened to you, Evie?"

Takari's lulling tone floated into my mind, scattering my thoughts as I splashed cold water on my face. Combing my fingers through my hair, I tamed the loose strands and wove them in a tight braid. "What do you mean?" I asked, but not unkindly.

Many events had taken place over the year since I'd met Takari, and while I considered her—and Romulus—as my first friends, I'd grown up since meeting them. Their noble ideas about the world and goals rose in sharp contrast with mine, although I sensed Takari wasn't referencing the past year, but what had happened with Jezebel.

"You've changed," Takari explained, shaking

drops of water from her brown skin, the dark blue patterns glittering in a whirl of beauty on her arms. "You used to be young, hopeful and so willing to help others but now. . ." she trailed off, unsure how to frame her next words.

I sensed the insult and stiffened before cupping my hands and letting tension roll off my shoulders. It was a technique I'd learned in the Meditation Meadows, to remain open to conversation and avoid leaping to conclusions based on what I assumed someone might say. I needed to wait and let their thoughts flow, keeping my peace and answering accordingly. "Speak your mind, Takari. I will not be angry with you."

Leaning back on her ankles, Takari stared at the sparkling stream. The clear waters were shallow enough to wade across, and on the other side, scattered trees and shrubs—budding with the first flowers of spring—hid the landscape. Since leaving the Crystal Forest, we'd followed the stream deeper into a valley with shaded trees and tall boulders, as though the wood had a secret it was intent on keeping.

"You're different Evie, tough, and you don't have as much empathy as you used to. I respected you for that trait and how driven you were to find your mother and assist the kingdom of men. I won't deny you've had some hard times. We all have, but you shouldn't let it lead you down a dark road of no return."

My fingers snarled in a knot, and I yanked my hair, creating an impossible tangle. Regardless, I finished my braid and tossed it behind my back with more vehemence than I intended. I'd promised Takari not to be angry with her, and yet resentment surged like a wave of bile. Closing my eyes momentarily, I sucked in air through my parted lips to give myself time to let the right words rise. "Are you referring to Adomos? The sword? Or Jezebel's death?"

"All of it, Evie." Takari waved her arms to emphasize her point, her dark eyes drilling into mine. "Every time something bad happens to you, you get a little more bitter and drawn inward because you let those situations define you. The struggles you face shouldn't determine who you are. Although they shape and teach you. You haven't had the proper time to grieve for your losses, but you can choose who you become. Once we were all young and innocent, naïve, forced to grow up in Labraid. My people are gone, my lover has disappeared, and my baby is dead. My past is sad and thinking about it makes me weary, but what keeps me standing with my head held high is hope for the future. Evie, you have to hold onto hope to prevent the darkness from taking over, from making you resentful, and turn toward revenge. No one starts out evil, but when you let darkness take root in your heart, and allow the seed of hatred to be planted, it becomes more difficult to decipher good from evil. You have a heart and a conscious, remember to listen to that inner voice that helps us distinguish between good and evil. Evie, you also have the red sword—against my recommendation—you slew a goddess, and now you travel with a half-demon. One of those is enough to drive one mad. I'd rather you be the savior of the kingdom of men than the one who falls into darkness. But the path you choose is up to you. I wouldn't be a good friend if I didn't speak my mind and warn you."

Staring intently at the bushes across the water, I bit my bottom lip, a strong aversion rising within me. "How do you do it?" I choked out. "Killing Jezebel was supposed to make me feel better, and it did. It does! But it awoke something within me, an awareness of my power, and I'm not sure what to do with it. I want to have hope. I want to make the right choices, but everything I've done in the past has led me here. After all this time, I've learned so much, but I still don't have answers. I'm certain the key is my father and after I find him, I'll know."

Takari squeezed my arm, her next words as gentle as the faint breeze. “You’re still following the plan your mother set out for you, aren’t you? You learned magic, took the red sword, and now you’ll meet with the defenders and go find your father. Along the way, perhaps you’ll find the answers you seek.”

I sighed, staring at the waters, the question burning in the back of my throat. “Do you believe I was born to take back the kingdom of men? To rule?”

“I can’t read the future and I’m not sure what will happen, but your magic is strong. You are strong. I don’t want to see you defeated because you aren’t sure. Don’t lose your light, Evie.”

Swallowing hard, I nodded, wondering how the shift in my attitude was so obvious to her. Rising, I dusted off my legs. “We should get back. Romulus will wonder why we took so long.”

Takari stood, too. “Evie, it always helps to talk. I may not have all the answers, but I will promise to listen. Burdens are less heavy when shared with someone.”

I parted my lips to respond when the snap of a tree branch shattered the serenity. A flock of birds flew screeching overhead, startled by the thrashing in the underbrush. My heartbeat sped up as I squinted. Across the stream, dark shapes moved between the trees. It could have been a predator, a wolf, maybe a bear if they lived in these parts, but a cold shudder went down my spine. I stared a moment longer until Takari tugged at my arm. "Let's go," she whispered. "I'm not sure what's out there, but we should move on."

With one last glance over my shoulder, I followed her back to camp.

Romulus waited, mounted on one of the horses, his silver hair slicked back from his forehead. He assessed me briefly with his icy glare, making me wonder where we stood.

I'd told no one about the kiss Adomos and I shared after I killed Jezebel, and Adomos remained out of sight as we traveled. I sensed his presence when he was near and recalled the vow he'd made to me, my breath coming short and fast at the thought. We hadn't been alone together since that night and conflicted emotions chased through my thoughts. I wanted to taste his lips on mine again, but I couldn't forget his warning. "You will make many enemies with me by your side."

And then there was the problem of the red sword. I kept it tied to my back and wrapped in a cloth, but still, I heard its bloodthirsty voice ever so faintly. *Kill. Kill. Kill.* As if the last death hadn't been enough. It would only be a matter of time before the urge swelled and grew and I'd want to take up the sword and strike and kill until it was sated. Romulus had warned me about it, but he hadn't been against it like Takari, which made me wonder why. When the opportunity arose, I'd take the time to clear the air between us and ask his opinion.

"We heard something out there." I pointed back toward the stream. "It frightened off the birds. Are there trolls in these parts?"

"I'm not aware of any." Romulus shrugged. "Wild animals live in this wood. Perhaps you saw one of them."

I crossed my arms, brow furrowing at the way Romulus belittled the fact that something was out there. As I considered the shadow I'd seen, the more certain I became that it wasn't an animal at all. However, after the demise of Jezebel, I assumed everything in the wood was full of malice.

"We should go." Romulus gestured for Takari and me to mount up. "The Hall of Defenders is nearby. We should reach their haven by evening if we make haste."

A sensation of numbness washed over me as I mounted up, the horse's back warm between my thighs. Conflict arose in my mind, two thoughts warring with each other. I'd grown up sleeping outside, living in a tent, and bathing in the wild, but my stay at Anon Loam had shown me how extraordinary life could be indoors, in man-made or elf-made dwellings. Magic had quickened within me, allowing me to grow into a mage while my skills with hand-to-hand combat had lessened. I'd grown soft and couldn't deny the longing to sleep in a snug bed tonight, even though reaching the Hall of Defenders left me feeling defensive.

During my stint in the Hills of Elsdore, Romulus had extended the invitation for me to join the defenders, but it had been ill-timed. After Jezebel tortured me, I wanted to recoil away from the world and go where no one could hurt me. The elven haven of Anon Loam was ideal until I learned magic and a restlessness seized me. Life was more than hiding and I needed a purpose which I'd gain as soon as I spoke with my father, the god Dagda.

Stealing a glance at Takari, who rode in front of me, I had to admit, she was right about me. I acted like one of the centaurs I'd grown up with, Larne. She had an attitude worse than Niamh, except Larne did not take correction well. When the elders reproached her for anything, no matter how minor, she stomped into the woods and came up with a petty prank to satisfy her rage. She was weak and selfish, and her inability to take correction was childish. I imagined her life must be miserable, but it was solely her fault. Takari's warning was a glaring reminder of what I could become. That and the sordid memory of the red sword slurping up Jezebel's ashes.

Lost in thought, I didn't notice we'd stopped until Romulus's curse rang out. My horse jolted to a stop so quickly I slumped over its neck in surprise.

"What madness is this?" Romulus's tone was hard as he dismounted.

"What is it?" I asked, craning my neck. I was in the back and it was impossible to see over Takari, who gave a sharp cry and averted her eyes.

My fingers itched as I swung off my mount, ready to call up a ball of fire should there be trouble. Following Romulus, I skirted the horses and immediately stepped back, hand over my mouth at the horror that lay on the road.

The wind shifted, and the smell slammed into my nostrils, the scent of rot and dung so potent my eyes watered. A body lay in the road, human from what was left of it, the torso ripped open, blood and guts spilling across the ground. The crimson flow was dark as mud, the eyes socket-less. Someone had killed this person and then left them where the wild animals could nip at their body.

I closed my eyes, but it was already too late. The

hiss of the sword thrilled through me and its iron will synced with mine. Even though the body had been festering for a day, maybe more, the sword wanted to feast at death. I stumbled back to the horse. Resting my hands on the reins, I took deep breaths, knowing I had to control the sword. I didn't want Takari's bad omen about it to come true.

"I can't tell whether it's he or she, but we should bury them," Romulus decided. "They are wearing the livery of the defenders, cut down while returning home, but why and who were they fleeing from? All signs of a pack are gone and I don't see any wounds from an arrow, but there are claw marks. . ."

Trailing off, Romulus went silent while I calmed my racing heartbeat. Once I was no longer looking at the body, the voice of the sword was easier to control, but the scent of decay gagged the air with its deathly stink.

Romulus was quiet for so long that I dared to peek over at him. When I lifted my head, he was staring at me, a weary look on his face. My heart sank even before he spoke. "Evie, you need to find Adomos."

The blame was written across his face, ice in his expression. Romulus would always dislike Adomos, hate him, even. After all, he was a half-demon, even

I had to admit that. The warning about Adomos and his dark side came back to me and my spine went rigid. "Just because someone is dead doesn't mean he did it."

Romulus's expression turned stony. "Why don't you go ask and see what he says?"

With that, he spun on his heel, facing the body again.

Takari spoke up. "Evie, he might know more about what is happening. His senses are keener than ours."

Once again, she was right, and I'd leaped to a conclusion. I backed away from the horses and the road, a sinking sensation humming in my gut. "I'll search the woods for him and catch up with you later."

2

The woods appeared normal as I stumbled into the underbrush, using my tracking skills to mark a path back to the road. It was fortunate I grew up in the forest. Even though this one was different, I'd learned about marking a path and looking for clues to find my way back home. Swallowing hard, I followed my senses, letting my magic attune to Adomos. A rush of sensation went through me, a twisting in my gut, a dryness in my mouth.

"Adomos," I called out, too afraid to shout, but wanting him to know I was nearby and searching for him.

A rustling in the thicket made me hesitate, revealing nothing more than a rabbit that dived back into the underbrush when it saw me. Pausing, I licked a finger and held it up to the wind, wondering which direction to continue in. A faint scent of rot carried to my nostrils. I wrinkled my nose and moved in that direction. It came again, the potent scent of death and decay. A sixth sense warned me it wasn't a wounded animal. More people were dead.

Clenching my fists, I refused to believe Adomos was to blame, although I knew little about his past or even his habits. I'd seen the fire in his eyes when he kissed me, but beyond knowing he'd helped me heal from Jezebel's torment, little else had passed between us. It wasn't for a lack of trying; it was simply the fact that he wasn't open about his past, believing it would do no good to discuss it.

Now the seed of doubt Romulus had planted itched at me. What did Adomos hunt and eat?

"Evie. You shouldn't be here."

His low voice rolled through me, sending my skin tingling. My apprehension faded, replaced with want. I tilted my head to take in his height and breadth, my eyes lingering rather too long on his naked torso. Adomos preferred not to wear clothes, leaving his chest exposed and his wings on display. Although he stood in the shadows, a glint of light caught the golden runes which covered his dark blue skin and highlighted the gleam of pale eyes. His feet were planted, widespread, arms crossed as he faced me and then turned, jerking his head downhill.

Stepping to his side, I followed his movements and stiffened. The hills rolled down into an embankment, displaying the void of a cave. Before it, bodies littered the ground. A small party of ten caught off guard and slaughtered in the valley. I guessed the body Romulus was burying belonged to this group. Perhaps they had run for help but only got so far when they were brutally cut down.

This time I wasn't able to look away from the slaughter and my mind buzzed with the voice of the sword. Worst of all, I had no desire to suppress it. My fingers tingled at the sight of so much blood and death, and for a moment, I was lost in a haze of bloodlust.

Adomos's hand lay heavy on my shoulder as he shook me. "Evie."

Blinking, I snapped out of the haze, reluctantly tearing my gaze from the carnage to meet his golden glare.

"It's the sword, isn't it?" he asked.

I nodded. "I hear it speaking in my head, but I can control it." The half-truth slipped out easily because I didn't want him looking at me with pity or trying to help me escape what I'd done to myself. My thoughts ventured back to Takari's words, insinuating that I could let myself become a monster if I didn't keep my hope and empathy. Changing the topic, I gestured to the bodies. "What happened here?"

"I don't know, but there's an unusual scent here and movement in the cave beyond. Whoever did this isn't gone yet. Maybe one of the attackers was wounded and is in the cave, trying to recover."

I frowned. "But who would commit such an act?"

"It is apparent that whoever did this had no honor, maybe bandits or mercenaries. Bandits are more loyal to each other, but mercenaries are ruthless. If anyone gets in their way, even from their own number, they will not hesitate to cut them down."

He didn't say the other options I was thinking; that it could be the work of squads sent out from the capital. Such a squad had wiped Takari's people out, leaving her homeless while her people fled as refugees to Anon Loam and other havens.

I scratched the back of my neck, thinking of a blade slicing through exposed skin. I needed—wanted—to do something about this because I was certain it wasn't Adomos's fault. However, I needed an explanation for Romulus and Takari. We had our differences, but I considered them friends and didn't want them to turn against me. They were good people and had taken me in during my time of need.

"What were you going to do before I showed up?" I asked.

"Investigate the cave."

"I'll come with you," I volunteered and waited for Adomos to dissuade me from joining him.

"Keep your magic ready," he said.

Pleasantly surprised, I cupped my hands, ready to summon a ball of fire if needed, and followed Adomos down the grassy hill into the valley. Sparse trees towered above us, letting in plenty of sunlight but hiding those who might be on the surrounding hillock. A falcon flew overhead, pulling my eyes upward. Shoulders tense, I stepped carefully, trying to avoid staring at the mangled bodies.

As we walked, the call of the sword pulsed within, dark and hungry. Sweat dripped down my neck as I ignored the lure, breathing shallowly out of my mouth to keep the smell from infiltrating my senses. I couldn't lose control in front of Adomos.

Pale sunlight lit up the entrance of the cave, the opening surrounded by stones and thick bushes. A tunnel led in; the ceiling so low Adomos would have to bend over to enter. A sudden boldness came over me, a desire to be useful, and I summoned a ball of fire into the palm of my hand. "I'll look."

"Let me go first." Adomos's deep voice rumbled as he moved past me, stooping to avoid hitting the ceiling.

I wanted to bristle, but I didn't. I was a princess, half goddess, trained as a warrior and a mage. Still, Adomos had the right to be protective. He'd sworn to serve me and in the past, my ignorance had forced me to rely on others. I used to be bold and brave—for example when I saved Takari—but that was before I'd met my mother and Jezebel had tortured me. Now, a sensation of adventure gripped me as we moved inside. The musty air in the cave blocked the stench of death, making me believe Adomos was right. If someone was inside, they were hidden or licking their wounds, although there was no sign of bloodshed or fighting.

The tunnel opened up into a cavernous hollow, cracks in the ceiling letting in a thin stream of filtered sunlight. Adomos stood up straight, and I held up the flame to lighten the darker crevices. The cave stretched up, and I wondered if we'd traveled under the hill. The way the cavern expanded reminded me of Adomos's lair in Elsdore, but instead of seeing passageways twisting away into blackness, there was nothing but solid rock that met my eyes.

"There's no one here," I whispered, keeping my voice low, just in case.

"No, but I still sense something unusual," Adomos said.

I waited a beat, growing dread threading through my veins. The skin on the back of my neck prickled, acknowledging a hidden menace. A slight tremor beneath my feet knocked me off balance. I threw out my arms as Adomos hissed and stepped back.

I stepped further into the cave as a crack split the ground.

"Evie, come back this way," Adomos shouted.

The crack widened as he held out his arms for me. I leaped, intending to cross the fissure, but the ground opened up and swallowed me whole.

3

The feeling of weightlessness was terrifying as I fell, down, down, down, arms flailing, hands reaching but unable to use my magic to halt my downward trajectory. Worst of all, above me was nothing but darkness and the sound of a clink as if someone had closed the opening in the rock. An impossible feat. With Adomos on the other side of the cave, and myself at the bottom, it was clear we'd walked into a clever trap.

I landed with a thump on a mossy stack of pallets, soft enough to cushion my fall and keep me from breaking bone, but still hard enough to knock all the air out of my body. The scabbard of the sword cut in my back but, unable to breathe, I closed my eyes and let the wave of pain pass over me. When I caught my breath, I sat up, chest heaving, and took in my surroundings.

Torches burned on the concave walls, revealing rows of barrels and a tunnel twisting out of sight. The air was dry, smelling of nothing worse than mud, leading me to assume I'd landed in some kind of underground storage room. Standing, I wrinkled my brow in confusion and a voice floated to my ears.

"When the hunter catches his prey, he plays with it before he eats, and you will be a delicious feast."

Stifling a scream, I spun around, ready to hurl a ball of fire, but the man who leaned against the wall made me drop my hands. My mouth went dry as I stared at him. Clothed in shadows, he appeared like a king of darkness, black hair falling to his shoulders, cheekbones sharp enough to slice through skin, ears that ended in a point. But it was his eyes that arrested me. Deep pools of soullessness as his gaze raked down my body, leaving me feeling as though, even in my armor, I wasn't wearing enough clothing.

A cloak shrouded the rest of his appearance and as he pushed off from the wall, his height forced me to tilt my head up. He was almost as tall as Adomos, but lean instead of brawny, and the power of his presence was almost overwhelming. Using my abilities, I sensed the undercurrent of powerful magic that emitted from him. Who was he?

When he took a step toward me, I lifted my hands again. "Stay back."

A low chuckle came out of his throat. "Or else?"

I summoned a ball of fire and let it hover above my palm. Raising an eyebrow, I waited.

"Ah. You intend to burn me, but let's see if you can hit me."

He took another step, and I aimed the fire at his legs. He spun, his cloak whirling around him like a shield, sending sparks dancing as my fireball missed. I readied another and tossed it at his chest, but he bent backward and let it slam into the wall behind him. Stepping back, I threw another ball and readied my magical shield. As expected, he dodged the third one too, yet did not retaliate, leaving me questioning whether he had magic or was simply nimble at evading it.

I held up my magic shield, and he spun one more time, sending a wind roaring toward me. It hurled me against the wall, the shield faded and my sword cut into my sore back again. Cold fingers closed around my neck and I brought my knee up, but he leaned away from me. As I lifted my hands, his fingers closed around my wrists, yanking my hands over my head. He pressed his body up against me, pinning me against the wall as he stared down at me, his face so close I tasted his breath.

Overcome by fury, I tried to shake him off, but he'd pinned me tight. I regretted not grabbing the sword when I had the chance. Oddly, its voice remained silent, as though the fall had snapped the thread between the sword and I.

"So, you're the warrior princess," my captor said, his breath sending a wave of mint with the light tang of smoky tobacco.

I glared at him. "You know who I am, but who are you?"

His soulless eyes danced with mischief. "The truth will evade you for a time. I came to see who my enemy is, but you're not as docile and weak as Jezebel led me to believe."

"Jezebel is dead," I snapped, and then because I couldn't resist, I added. "I killed her."

He shrugged. "Pity. She was amusing, but she had to die sometime. It was clear she underestimated you, a mistake I won't be making."

A surge of hidden magic tingled around me like the subtle strands of a spider's web. He'd confirmed his status as one of my enemies, and this glimmer of magic I sensed warned me he was much stronger than Jezebel. I should have drawn the sword and killed him without question, but when his eyes lingered on my mouth, I wondered what else he wanted. "I have friends in the area," I warned him. "They will come looking for me should you attempt to hold me here."

"Wrong assumption again. I don't intend to hold you here. I only wanted to meet you on my own terms, where no one else would interfere."

"If you just want to talk, let me go."

He made a clicking sound with his tongue. "You've already tried to burn me, and I have no desire to face your sword. Yes, I know what it is too. Claíomh Dearg. The Red Sword. The queen of men took it before I could get my hands on it, and now it answers to you."

His words offered a clue to who he was, and my mind raced at his words. "Is that what you've come for, the sword?"

"Once, I desired it, but now I have everything, even the location of the survivors, the last royal bloodline of the kingdom of men. Interesting how the queen stayed concealed for so long, and then you appeared and led Jezebel to her hiding place. My spies, quick to gather information, alerted me to what had happened. Your torture in Elsdore and then sheltering in Anon Loam. How curious."

He spoke so evenly and smoothly, my blood ran cold at his words. My vision tunneled. He not only knew who I was; he knew my every movement. He didn't want the sword, but I was certain he wanted me dead, even though his words said otherwise. Why else track my movements? My lips parted as my breath came shallow, but he continued.

"I know the Queen of the Elves kept the sword in her haven and we made a deal, a deal you might be aware of. She protected the red sword, and I promised not to attack her people."

I closed my eyes, recalling the queen's warning against taking up the sword. Had I listened to her wisdom? No, at the time I thought she was bullying me, with her beautiful grace and magic that combed through my mind. She didn't have the right to read my thoughts, but I'd never questioned why she forbade me from taking up the red sword. I assumed she had nefarious intentions when, in actuality, she'd made a deal to protect her people. Which meant…no, it couldn't be possible. Was the man holding me captive the angel of death? The tyrant who'd taken the kingdom of men from my mother, Queen Ceana Mor, and the man who was not my father, King Conan Mor?

Opening my eyes, I examined him. Kedron Abbadon. Was it possible that it was him? If so, he was ageless, immortal, a demon in human form, and I was no match for his wit. The fear must have shown on my face because his brightened, the darkness chased by away and replaced with something maddening. Glee.

"It's not possible," I whispered, wanting him to confirm the truth. "You can't be the angel of death. He rules over the kingdom of men, far from here, and he's. . ." I trailed off, unwilling to let the insult leave my lips and invite his wrath.

"What? Ancient? Interesting that you judge me and not the Nephilim you travel with."

My face burned. "He's different."

Kedron Abbadon grinned, displaying a sharp row of teeth. I flinched back on instinct, heart racing as he spoke. "No one is different. They are all predictable. If I wanted, I could use him, but he's suffered enough. I'm much more curious about you."

"Why? Aren't you going to kill me and take the sword?"

"Tempting." He glanced at the hilt of the sword before studying my face again. "But after I made a deal with the elven queen, I lost interest in it. I no longer need it to achieve my goals, but you need it to achieve yours. At least, if you know what you want."

His fingers tightened around my neck, squeezing for just a moment, tight enough to cut off my breath. His face inched closer to mine. "Do you know what you want?"

I glared back at him, drowning in his dark eyes. His question brought up my own insecurities about who I was, what my mission was, and why I was alive. I knew what Queen Ceana Mor had wanted for me, and the elven queen, and even the centaurs in the wood. Although their hopes for me were purer, wishing me well in the hopes that I could find the place where I belonged. I was supposed to fight Kedron Abbadon, who held me by the throat and take the kingdom from him.

If I could breathe properly, I would have laughed at the irony. I was young and untested and even though I'd accessed my magic in Anon Loam, now I wrestled with a sword that wanted to control me. Conversely, Kedron Abbadon was strong and experienced. Any war strategy I crafted would be impossible to complete with him tracking me, spying on me, and sensing my every move. He even knew where the stronghold of the defenders was, and—if I escaped him by some miracle—I had to warn them. They weren't safe.

"No, you don't know, do you? I'll tell you what you want."

Letting go of my neck, he tilted my chin up and brushed his mouth against mine. Shocked, I parted my lips, overcome by the way he held my arms above my head, his hard body pressing against me and the warmth of his mouth consuming mine. It was nothing like the kiss I'd shared with Adomos and even though Kedron was my enemy, the longing within me to be held and loved made me respond.

I kissed him back, my mind reeling at just how delicious his lips tasted. My stomach fluttered, a groan rose in my throat and when he slid his tongue into my mouth, I welcomed his claiming.

He pulled back, eyes sparkling as he studied my lips. "Curious," he said, voice low.

Did he sense it too? The connection? The way my heart pounded and blood roared in my ears. I wanted him to kiss me again, and I hated myself for it, trying to banish what had just happened from my mind. When he hooked a finger under the band of my pants, I gasped. "Please don't."

He paused and moved his lips right next to the shell of my ear. "Are you a virgin? Do you imagine I would take that from you? There's no time now. Your bodyguard will search for you and your friends will wonder where you are. No one will believe the bodies on the road are my doing. They will blame the Nephilim, the defenders will mistrust you, and you'll invite many enemies, including my armies. I've sent my elite warriors into the wood to cause chaos. I've been untested for so long, no one dares rise and cross my path. Not even you. But I'm ready for some excitement. You are my prey, but I will not kill you now. I'm going to let you live, but first I must leave you with my mark. When you grow disgusted with this world, drained of fighting, come to my kingdom, come find me and you can be my queen."

Queen? When I tried to look at him, to gauge if I'd heard correctly, he spun me around so quickly that my face hit the wall. He yanked my shirt up, baring my skin to him. I suppressed a whimper as something cold slipped around my wrists, immobilizing me against the wall. My immediate reaction was to pull against it and free my arms, but the bonds held me tight. I wanted to lash out and kick back at him, but shame and anger kept me still.

"I don't want you following me, especially with that sword," he cooed, holding my shirt up with one hand while the other grazed my skin.

My hips jerked at his touch, and he tightened his grip. I squeezed my eyes shut, waiting for him to take me, claim me, ruin me.

4

Teeth sank into my side and my entire body went stiff. A bolt of pain shot up my spine as his powerful jaws clamped down again. Harder this time. I bit my lip to keep from crying out because I sensed that was what he wanted, to invoke pain, to hear me scream. I would not give him the pleasure.

When he removed his mouth, blood and saliva pooled from my wound and while the pain subsided, it still pulsed through my veins. Kedron ran his hands over my bottom before pressing himself against me. His breath feathered my ear. "I'm going to leave you like this, princess, and you'll come to me when you're ready."

Anger boiled, forcing me to spit my words at him. "I'll never join you or become your queen."

He chuckled again. "I only meant you'll come when you're ready to kill me, but should you change your mind, I will enjoy making you my dark queen. The kingdom of men was taken from you, and by rights, you're the firstborn. You should rule. I alone have the power to give back what was taken."

"You're the one who took it first and I would betray everything I believe in if I trusted you."

"You assume too much. I never asked for your trust."

His mouth nipped at my ear, and I flinched away.

"Your anger betrays you. Go on, pretend that you didn't enjoy our kiss. I know the truth about you, and the secret of your birth. You aren't human, not fully. You're a goddess, and that sets you above all others in this world. One day you'll understand that you are better and don't need to bow to the people of Labraid or keep to the old ways. You can set a fresh path for yourself, become more than a warrior, and I can help you achieve it all. One question halts your journey, and I can help you discover your identity and find your purpose."

"No," I said firmly. How did he guess? It was as though my mind was laid bare before him, as easy to read like an open book. But I didn't feel his magic anymore. In fact, I sensed nothing, as though we were in a void.

"Remember my words," he said and slid something cold into my hand. "Here is the key to your bonds. I won't have you follow me or try to kill me. When you figure out to escape, take the tunnel on the right and you'll find yourself in the wood again. I have given you life, but should you run into my warriors, they will not hesitate to kill you."

"Next time, I will not hesitate to kill you," I retorted.

Silence met my ears.

I tilted my head back as far as I could, but he was no longer beside me and the power of his presence had vanished. The weight in the air was gone and my mind was clear again. What was even more concerning was that I hadn't noticed the effect he had on me until he was gone. And that kiss.

No, I couldn't think about the kiss. I had to focus on freeing myself and chasing him down. Craning my neck, I studied the silver object in my hand, a key to the chains he'd closed around my wrists. It was but the work of a moment and with some concentration, I was free again. I tugged my shirt down over the messy bite he'd given me and pulled the red sword free.

A roar filled my ears, the hum of battle and blood. Instead of taking the left path, as instructed, I took the right tunnel and dashed down it, while torch light flickered on either side. The path led down, and the air was thick with stink. I kept my eyes wide, sure it would be impossible for him to disappear. Unless he ran as well, I'd catch up with him at any moment. Unless. . .

I slowed to collect my thoughts. I'd acted out of impulse and anger, and that was the best way for a warrior to be led astray. It was possible that Kedron Abbadon had tricked me again, urging me to take the left tunnel to escape, when it was his plan to take that route all along. Frustrated at myself for underestimating my opponent, I spun around and crashed into a hard body.

The impact knocked me off guard, and I bounced back, slamming against the wall. Before I had the presence of mind to bring the sword up, whoever I'd hit punched a fist into my stomach. I bent over, wheezing for air, at the same time searching for my magic. Heat boiled in my belly as my attacker lashed out, kicking me off my feet. I landed heavily on my side, hurling the ball of fire as I went down.

He grunted at the impact and I lifted the sword, in a matter of seconds taking in an armored beast with glittering eyes. Furry hair stuck out from his arms and legs, his eyes were slitted like a wolf and although the rest of his features were covered with a helmet and other armor, I knew I did not fight a mere man, but one of Kedron Abbadon's elites.

Letting my rage build into energy, I thrust with the sword. He dogged and again I was surprised by the lack of connection from the sword, but I didn't let it deter me. My training from years ago made my movements instinctive. I lunged onto the offensive, striking at his feet, stabbing at his chest, and then swinging at his neck. Skillfully, he danced away from my movements, fists at the ready to punch when the opportunity arose. The momentum of the sword carried me forward, and I snarled as my sword struck his armor. The clang reverberated through me, making my arm numb. Gritting my teeth, I struck again as his fist flew out and punched me in the cheek. I heard something in my face crack as my back struck the wall. I grunted, aware I'd have matching bruises on my spine and face. By the time I regained my feet, the elite warrior was gone.

The thump of footsteps echoed in the tunnel. With a curse, I sheathed the sword, aware the centaurs of Beluar would be appalled with my behavior. After my ordeal today, I was past caring what they thought, and with a pang, I recalled I needed to find Adomos and return to Romulus and Takari. Would they believe my tale? Chasing after

Kedron Abbadon had been a terrible idea after he'd been thoroughly prepared for our first encounter. I resolved myself to train harder, better, and become faster. The next time we met, he would not best me.

Returning to the storage room, I took the left tunnel, as he'd told me, and walked uphill, out of the cave, and into sunshine. As my eyes became accustomed to the light, I assessed my situation. I'd come up above the bodies, the breeze whispering as it blew clean air toward me. Still, I tensed, readying my magic in case more elites swarmed the woods. This was likely the way Kedron Abaddon had come. If I'd followed his directions, I might have been able to catch up with him, but it was likely he assumed I'd be too full of fury to escape.

I bit my lower lip and crouched low. I was uphill and below me was the back of the cave and the bodies, but no sign of Adomos. Closing my eyes, I allowed my mind to reach for him, trying to establish a connection. But nothing happened. Whatever had transpired in the cave had done something to my senses. Was I under a spell? I'd have to ask Takari.

Taking one last look around for Adomos, I decided to return to my friends. Adomos could take care of himself, and Romulus and Takari were in greater danger if the elites attacked them.

My heart constricted at the thought of them being attacked, and I set off in a run.

5

The silence of the wood was sinister as I dashed around the sparse trees back to the road. The dirt beneath my feet was churned and my heart sank as I spun to the left and right, seeing no sign of the horses, my companions, or the dead body. Tilting my head skyward, I reajusted my position according to the direction we'd been traveling in and jogged down the road, heart in my throat. It wasn't until I passed a mound of dirt that I began to worry. Bright red blood stained the area, and arrows poked out of the soft dirt.

On instinct, I moved off the road and ducked behind a tree. It was clear my companions had been attacked, likely by elite warriors, as Kedron Abbadon toyed with me in the cave. I raked my mind, trying to recall what Romulus had said about the defenders. We were on the road, but they were hidden nearby, and we'd reach the place by midnight. I guessed they had to be in some sort of fortress or mountain.

Pressing my hand to my forehead, I tried to shake off Kedron's face, his dark eyes, sinister smile, and those teeth, all sharp and strong. He aimed to mess with my head, sway my choices, and now I was alone, but not helpless. A dark thought struck me that if I found Adomos, I could sneak off and start making my way across the country to Dun'gilly Mountain, where supposedly my father lived. I banished that thought because a sudden determination rose in me. I wouldn't leave my friends to the torture of Kedron Abbadon and his armies.

A thin voice carried to my ears, and I spun around, my eyes widening as I took in the appearance of a girl, only a few years younger than I. Her hair was braided across one shoulder like mine and something about her appearance rang of familiarity. "Reish?" I asked.

"Yes, it is I," she confirmed.

I schooled my expression to be blank as I studied her. Reish, the seer, only appeared in a time of need and her appearance changed based on my maturity level. Now she only appeared slightly younger than

I, which was an improvement from when she appeared as a child. Questions tumbled out of my mouth. “Why are you here? Do you know where Romulus and Takari went? Have you seen Adomos?”

Her round eyes widened at the pace of my questions, and she lifted a hand. “I am here to warn you, Evie. All is not what it seems. Friends turn to enemies, enemies turn to friends, you’ll need to be careful as you continue to the Hall of Defenders. Use your best judgment on whom to trust.”

My mouth went dry and, keeping my voice low, I forced the next words out. “I met the angel of death. Is that why you’re warning me? He’s not what I expected.”

“Evie, I can’t advise you, only warn you of the shifting visions I see. Meeting him has clouded your judgment. Perhaps it was what he intended, to slow your mind, to make you believe the lies he fed you. A time will come for you to mull over his words, but that time is not now. The woods are full of warriors, the Hall of Defenders is near, and your companions are in grave trouble. Find them. Protect them. I must go.”

“Wait, which direction?” I begged, not wanting to be left alone with my thoughts again.

“You were forest bred and born. Use your tracking skills.”

With those final words, she was gone, blending through the long shadows the trees cast until she was gone.

Kneeling, I examined the ground beside me, squinting against the light until I was rewarded with a bead of blood and a footprint. I followed, noting the horse's hooves, and more blood. My chest tightened at the amount of blood on the ground and flecking the leaves. I could only hope it was one of the warriors, but considering the armored one I fought in the cave, that likelihood was low.

"Evie?"

"Takari?"

She poked her head out of a hedge, her gaze darting across the area before she beckoned to me. As I neared, I took in the tightness of her posture, the fear in her eyes. A cold wave of fear went through me. "What happened? Where is Romulus?"

Pressing her lips together, she gave just a tiny shake of her head before the story came pouring out, her words tumbling over each other in her haste. "I did the best I could to bandage his wound. The bleeding has stopped now, but Evie, it's bad. Tall warriors in heavy armor came out of the woods and attacked us. It was an ambush. They beat us back, killed one horse, and stabbed Romulus in the side. They would have killed us, but something distracted them. I think the attack was called off."

Her blue magic sparked, and I squeezed her arm. "I was attacked too, Takari. We need to get out of these woods. How close is the Hall of Defenders?"

She frowned. "A hard day's ride. I don't think Romulus will make it in his condition."

"May I see him?" I asked. Ever since I'd met Romulus, he'd been hard, invincible in my mind, a well-seasoned warrior and a traveler. Nothing took him by surprise, and I'd never seen him weak or in need.

Takari led me into the hedge, where a low groan came to my ears. Romulus sat propped against a bush, holding his side. Blood covered his shirt, and I stepped back in alarm. "I can make it," he rasped. "Tie me to you and let the horse have its head. If we stay a night in these woods, we'll be dead before daybreak."

Those words made me move. Romulus was little help, already weak from blood loss, but I managed to get him on the horse and swung up behind him to keep him from falling.

"I'll lead the way," Takari volunteered in a trembling voice.

"Is there anything we can do? Cloaking magic to keep us concealed?" I asked as I leaned against

Romulus, aware that if it had been six months ago, I would have been desperate to be close to him like this. My fingers gazed at his blood-stained shirt, and I jerked my hand away.

"I have nothing," Takari admitted.

I wished I were stronger in other areas of my magic, but my skill as a mage was for war. I could ward off attacks and protect others while Takari's magic enticed the truth out of people. Neither of us could cast a spell of concealment.

The horses set off through the thicket, their pace quickening as we reached the flat road again and galloped down it. Romulus groaned and leaned back against me, his weight heavy. I held him up as best I could while the horse swayed. I could only imagine how rough the ride was for Romulus with his wound.

I prayed to the gods as we dashed, hoping we'd arrive soon and this ordeal would be over. A flash of silver drew my gaze in the woods and my heartbeat sped up. Darkness hovered in those trees, a fog-like mist rising from the ground like a black cloud of evil coming to consume us. Unable to tear my eyes away, I stared at the silver and black, a group of elites silently watching our progress yet making no move to attack. Why?

With a pang, I recalled I'd lost Adomos, and they

might have captured him. Would Kedron Abbadon have a use for Adomos? He'd called him a bodyguard and the skin on my neck prickled. For the past six months, I'd decided I had a choice about whether I took up my birthright and became the warrior to take back the kingdom of men from the angel of death. It was a purpose I longed to forsake and turn my back on, but fate had caught up with me and I didn't have a choice now. The angel of death was coming for me, whether or not I fought.

6

By nightfall, we were high in the hills. The horses slowed to a walk as they climbed upward. Torches flamed the path, bright spots of cheer in the growing darkness. Romulus was slumped against me, passed out, his pulse growing weaker by the moment. My heart ached at the thought of losing him, of the death of yet another person I was close to. Even though I'd upset him by my choices, I didn't want him to die. Bitter weariness settled in my bones. I wanted to tell Takari to hurry, but I didn't have the strength to speak, and if the elites were following us, I didn't want voices to give us away.

Occasionally she clucked to her mount, encouraging it to continue its ascent while flames cast odd shadows on the road, making me jump and lick my lips.

"Oy," a low voice called, "who goes there?"

I stiffened while Takari reined in the horse, coming to a stop. "It is I, Takari, along with Romulus, who is gravely injured, and Evie Mor. We seek refuge in your halls."

"Takari? By the gods, why didn't you say so? Come on."

The voice stepped out of the shadows and held up a light, revealing a group of four humans with bows on their backs and spears in hand. The way they held themselves was regal yet friendly, unlike the elves of Anon Loam.

"We'll lead you in but stay quiet, as of late enemies have been in these parts, although you probably know that if Romulus is injured."

Takari dismounted, took the horse by the reins, and beckoned for me to follow. I stayed on the horse's back since Romulus's weight pinned me down. The four men surrounded us, leading us away from the road and down a path that was barely wide enough for the horses. Branches poked at me as we descended and then we were somewhere dark with stone walls. A tunnel, I guessed, cleverly hidden among the trees.

Doors opened and closed, light flared, and

suddenly came the scent of hay and the smell of horses. We'd entered a barn. One of the men held the reins of my mount and smiled up at me, his eyes solemn, his mouth pleasant. A twinge of familiarity pinched me, but I couldn't exactly place him. I tore my eyes away as voices called out instructions, and a flurry of activity filled the stables.

"Call the healer."

"Prepare a pallet."

"Take care of the horses."

"Find Nolani."

Amid the flurry, I was helped off the horse, and Romulus's stiff body was taken and placed on a pallet. Four men carried him away while I rubbed my numb arms and joined Takari. Warm blood stained my clothes and the scent of death lingered on me. I blinked back sudden tears of relief and weariness as Takari took my hand and squeezed it. The man who'd held my mount joined us and extended his arm. "May I escort you to the hall?"

I nodded, examining him a bit more as he led the way. He gave me a sly look. "I'm not sure if you remember me, Princess Evie, but I'm glad to see you're alive. After Jezebel attacked and killed the queen, we weren't sure who survived."

I stared at him. "Eion?"

"You remember," he said, a note of astonishment in his tone.

I nodded, recalling the guard who'd helped me fight off the trolls when Jezebel attacked. He'd been sympathetic, and although I hadn't spared him a thought since, he was the one person who treated me as I wanted to be treated. Aye, a princess, but he fought alongside me, acknowledging my strength without trying to protect me.

My weariness shifted as I addressed him. "It was so long ago, I always wondered what happened to you. . ." I trailed off, thinking of my four younger siblings drifting away on a boat, my mother ensuring they got away safely. A twitch of bitter jealously came over me. They'd escaped while I suffered.

"I always wondered what happened to you too," he said gently.

Takari squeezed my hand as though she would speak. But as we left the barn, others joined us. Instead of responding to Eion, my gaze was drawn upward. My mouth dropped as I took in the sheer size of a massive fortress hidden behind a shaft of rock. Towers sprung high, and we walked up a row of stairs lined with guards who nodded to us.

Double doors opened into a grand hall and my eyes widened as scents and sounds accosted me.

People roamed everywhere, men, women, and children, and long tables overflowed with food and ale. It was the most people I'd ever seen in one place, and not even in Elsdore had I seen this many humans. One by one, they grew quiet as we walked in and faces lifted, forks hung in mid-air, mugs were poised, suspended, as if under a spell as they stared at Takari and I.

A sinking sensation washed over me and suddenly I wanted to spin around and hide. But there was nowhere to go under the pressure of those gazes. A wave of dizziness washed over me, and I liked my dry lips. A man stood, a horned helmet on his head, his blonde beard in two braids going down to his waist. He clapped meaty hands together, and then another stood and did the same, and another and another.

Shocked, I listened to the applause, and I knew it wasn't for Takari and her return to the Hall of Defenders. It was for me, the lost princess who had finally come home. At long last, I was somewhere where the people actually wanted me and I didn't have to prove myself. But that knowledge brought about another, scarier thought. As I'd suspected on the road, these people wanted me to liberate them from the angel of death, and I had no choice but to comply.

"Hush, hush," a female voice piped up. "You're going to frighten her away."

A tall woman bustled out of her seat, dark hair drawn up in a crown around her head as she approached us. As she moved, the room descended into silence, making her raise her arms as though scolding unruly children. "Eat. Drink. We will discuss all in time."

Half a beat passed before someone clinked their mug against another, and the merry sounds of eating and drinking returned. Relief seeped through me as the woman approached, her round face open and friendly. She put out a hand and shook my own, her palms rough and chapped, fingernails short. "Welcome to the Hall of Defenders," she said. "I'm Nolani. My husband is out hunting, but he'd be pleased to know you've entered our halls."

Without giving me a chance to respond, she let go of my hand and beamed as she faced Takari. The two embraced and held each other for a long moment. When Nolani pulled back, tears pooled her forest green eyes. "Takari, I was certain you'd stay with the elves and I'm so pleased you've joined us, for no matter how long or short you know you are always welcome here."

"I am grateful for your kindness, but Nolani, you should know that we were attacked on the road.

Romulus was with us too, he was taken to the healer."

Nolani's brow knitted together. "That is foul news. I will go see to Romulus. Sit, eat, drink. Shadi will take you to the guest rooms. Tomorrow we can speak in depth about this. In fact, your coming is timely. The council has gathered to discuss the unrest that plagues the land. I'm afraid these attacks are only part of the greater problem. Darkness grows and some say that he's on the move, coming to finish what he started."

I tensed, unaware of the speculation and doubt crossing the minds of the people. "Who?" I said more sharply than I intended.

Nolani's eyes flashed, and then she gestured to two seats at a table. "The time for conversation will be soon. For now, rest, forget your troubles if only for tonight."

She walked away as plates of steaming food and mugs of ale were placed in front of Takari and me. My stomach growled with the reminder that I hadn't eaten almost all day and a wave of fatigue made my shoulders sag. Picking up a wooden spoon, I took a bite, chewing carefully at my face flared with pain. The bones weren't broken, only bruised from the fight in the cave, and eating brought up a dull ache. The food, however, was delicious, albeit, simple fare. Unlike the delectable food of the elven kingdom, this was wholesome, nourishing food meant to strengthen the body.

Noise resumed as we ate, although I noticed those close by peering at me, but when I lifted my head to meet their bold stares, they hid them behind ale and soup. When my ravenous appetite had subsided, I whispered to Takari. "How come you went to the elves when your people were attacked instead of coming here?"

Takari studied her soup; her face was suddenly blank. She sighed. "I was weary and simply wanted to rest. The elven queen allows it. Besides, that haven is better suited to my people. Here the walls are made of stone, there's work to be done, and the people often come and go. It is true that one can rest here, but this is a fortress of safety, not a land to dwell in."

I stared around the wide hall and began to understand. In Anon Loam, I was often outside, but here we were in the bowels of a mountain. "So, why now?" I asked, recalling Nolani's greeting to Takari. "What changed?"

"You changed." Takari faced me. "You decided to leave Anon Loam, and here is the next logical place for you to go. I'm grateful you came. Even though this is not what you want, I believe it is important for you to hear from the defenders and understand their needs before you quest for your father. It is a quest I would like to join you on, but given Romulus' state and what might be going on out there, I'm not sure how useful I'd be to you." Takari dropped her voice even lower. "Did you find Adomos?"

I froze. I hadn't seen Adomos after Kedron attacked me, and I wasn't sure what to share with the defenders. "It wasn't him if that's what you're asking," I said coldly.

"I know. Romulus was just being careful. Half demons have always been our enemy, and he doesn't believe that's likely to change. But Evie, I see wherever you go, you bring change. Perhaps times are changing and it is time for a new era to rise. There are many who want the old kingdom restored, but even more who don't. If you plan on retaking the kingdom, it is something we should know so that we can prepare to aid you."

I shook my head. "That's not what I want."

She squeezed my arm. "No, not right now. Well, come, I want to see how Romulus is doing."

Takari rose, and I pushed the bowl of food away, my stomach clenching as I thought of Romulus's wound and his weight against me. How could I have eaten when he was in an unknown state?

"Takari? Evie?" A slim girl with large blue eyes

swayed up to us, pressing a hand to her round belly, the telltale sign of the beginning of her pregnancy. "I'm Shadi, I'll take you to the guest rooms."

"We'd like to see Romulus first. Do you know where they've taken him?" Takari asked.

"Aye, he's in one of the guest rooms as well. Follow me."

7

Shadi led us out from the loud hall into a quieter section of the fortress. Stone walls loomed above us, wide enough for a horse and rider to gallop through undisturbed. Passageways ended in sharp curves and heavy double doors blocked entrances to other sections. I guessed the styling of the keep was meant for defense, and my skin prickled as we passed.

Takari was right. This wasn't a home or haven like Anon Loam. It was a fortress of defense, dark and gloomy, but safe from threats beyond the Hall of Defenders. Threats like Kedron Abbadon and his elites.

Shadi led us through thick doors with bars on either side. It scratched the back of my neck, my heart beating faster at the idea of being trapped inside the mountain. Even though I didn't sense magic, the weight of the mountain felt like a burden on my shoulders, determined to bring me down. The air was thick, almost sour, despite the fragrant candles on a shelf of supplies. Even the scent of lavender and peppermint could not overpower the stench of sickness.

A woman folding bandages nodded at us and jerked her chin toward an adjoining door. "If you're here to see Romulus, he's sleeping."

"Thank you Kenda, we'll keep it brief," Shadi said.

A low moan drifted to my ears as Shadi led us through, a finger pressed to her lips. I balled up my fists, glancing at Takari for comfort as we crept into the darkened room. A lantern hung by the door, casting a tiny pool of light, but not enough to disturb his sleep.

Romulus lay on a pallet, eyes closed. Even in the darkness, his skin was pale, a shine of sweat glistening on his brow. The healer had cut his shirt away and covered his nakedness with a thin blanket. Still, he turned his head from side to side, muttering and groaning as a fever took him.

I wrapped my arms around my waist and blinked hard, unsure of what to say or do. Seeing Romulus cut down and weak was a stark reminder of what I was up against. What we all were up against. I'd never seen him in a position of weakness. During the times we traveled together, he was strong, tall, and always presented himself as the leader. He was a ranger, had traveled the wilds and nothing had taken him down. Until Kedron Abbadon and his elites.

Takari went to him quickly, sat on a chair by the pallet, and took his hand in one of hers. Blue magic flared brightly before going out like a flame caught in the wind. Instead of looking at him, I tore my eyes away and rubbed my heel against the uneven stone. I squeezed my arms around my waist harder, and as I did, a sharp pain went through my side. It throbbed, and I gasped. The wound! I'd forgotten about the bite mark and suddenly my skin itched.

Even though I was in a place of healing, I didn't want to ask for help. It would draw undue attention to the wound and lead to questions about how I'd gotten it. Questions I wasn't ready to answer.

"Kenda," Takari called. "Tell us, how is he?"

Kenda appeared behind me, her voice low, and I realized she was older than I'd first thought. Her tone was soft, as though she were used to giving bad news. "The night will tell my lady," she replied. "If you like, you can sit with him through the night, it might bring him some peace."

The lump in my throat swelled, and I stared at her. "What do you mean, the night will tell? Isn't he on the mend?"

Kenda reached out to squeeze my arm then drew her hand back as though she thought better of it. Her gaze lingered on my bloodstained shirt then moved to the sword still wrapped and strapped to my back. I wondered if she had any inkling of what it truly was, although, disturbingly, I hadn't heard its voice since my encounter with Kedron Abaddon.

"We can only hope he'll mend. The blade that pierced him was poisoned, and it had some time to work in his body. I've done all I can, but without great magic, he might die unless he has the strength to push through. If you wish to sit with him through the night, I'll bring pallets. The bathhouse is nearby too. I'll have you called if he takes a turn for the worse."

"A bath would do us good." Takari rose. "Evie, would you like to go while I sit with him? Then you can take a turn with him while I bathe."

I did not want to be alone with him. Nor did I want to leave and bathe, but I had no choice. I nodded weakly. Shadi steered me away, and I followed in a daze. It was only when the sound of water filled my ears that I jerked out of my dream-like state. I'd entered a cavern where water flowed out of the mountainside into a natural pool.

"Do you need assistance?" Shadi asked.

I stared helplessly at the shimmering waters, trying to accept the fact that Romulus might be dying. When she asked again, I shook my head. "No, I'm sorry, it's been a long day."

"I understand," she said and pointed. "Towels are here. Leave your clothes and use one of the robes when you're done. I'll see about finding you some clothes." Making a face, she touched her belly. "Or I'll have someone come check on you soon."

After she left, I was alone with the calming sound of the waters. My thoughts raced as I stripped off my ruined clothes. Romulus might be dying, Kedron Abbadon had returned to haunt me, and I had to warn the defenders. I lay my daggers and the sword on the rock before diving into the pool and scrubbing at my skin with a pumice stone.

This wasn't what I wanted. I hadn't chosen to come to the Hall of Defenders or meet with those who saw me as a tool to take back the kingdom of men and save them from the angel of death. But I didn't have a choice. It would be arrogant and foolish of me to turn my back on their needs, especially when I'd met him and knew what he wanted: to destroy. And I'd taken up the sword, found magic, and could fight him indirectly. A nudge in the back of my mind told me the key to discovering myself and my identity was finding my father. I needed answers from him. Why had he tricked my mother? What were his plans for Labraid? A conversation with him would direct my steps, and right now, I felt so alone.

I surfaced from the water, the coolness of it numbing my bruises, as a voice called my name. A voice I did not recognize until I turned around. "Evie?"

I made to rise out of the water and paused as I faced my sister.

8

It unsettled me how much she looked like our mother. Her face had the same bone structure, but instead of jet black hair, hers was dark brown and braided into an intricate weave that reached her waist. Unlike me, she was clad in a woolen dress. It was a reminder that it must grow cold under the mountain. Her chin trembled as she lifted her head, gray eyes assessing me.

I searched my memory for a name and came up with Brianna, the firstborn. Although Solane—our brother—might be her twin. In my bitterness regarding my siblings, I hadn't asked, hadn't wanted, to know more about them. I should have expected her presence since the guard, Eion, had told me they'd escaped, but seeing her in the bathing pools was unexpected. Had she waited until I was naked and vulnerable to approach me? It was likely Brianna didn't know about my magic, and I sank to my chin.

"Brianna," I said shortly.

Instead of coming closer, she placed a bundle of clothes—presumably for me—nearby and crossed her arms over her chest. Her expression and tone of voice gave away nothing as she asked. "Why are you here?"

I wanted to ask her the same question, and I searched the still waters for a response. "I came because Romulus and Takari asked me to, but I'm en route to elsewhere. Why are you here?"

Brianna narrowed her eyes. "Elsewhere? Does it mean you've come to help?"

I shrugged my shoulders then realized she couldn't see them under the water and added, "It depends."

She stilled, so calmly and queenly it reminded me of our mother, and it struck me that perhaps Brianna would make a good queen. But if she were queen, what did that make me?

"Mother always said that you were the warrior, the one who would take back the kingdom of men from the angel of death. But Mother is dead now and we are here, in the Hall of Defenders, trapped, just like we were underground. I've hidden my entire life, and I'm sick of it. I want to be free to walk the lands like you do."

The truth erased the streak of mounting jealousy, and I stared at her, understanding creeping across my mind like the rays of dawn awakening the sky. Brianna, Solane, Avalon, and Conan weren't free. Their royal blood made them prisoners, targets, just like me. Except I'd hidden with the centaurs and then again with the elves and now? A sudden boldness came over me. I had the upper hand here because I had something she wanted. Clearly, she'd come to propose a deal. I had to put aside my jealousy because it wasn't her fault that she'd benefited from growing up under our mother's care.

Lifting myself slightly out of the water, I rested my arms on the smooth stone of the floor and eyed her. "What do you want from me? Not what *Mother* wanted, what you want."

"I want to walk outside without fear of something taking off my head because of who I am."

I snorted.

She flinched, her steely gray eyes going darker. "Laugh if you will," she snapped.

I waved a hand. “I’m. . .that’s not what I meant. Someone will always want to capture and exploit us for who we are. I learned that after Jezebel captured me. The only way to live without fear is to figure out how to defend yourself. You have these walls, guards, and if you truly want to walk outside without fear, go live among the elves, as I did.”

This time it was Brianna’s turn to scoff at my words. “You went there to learn magic and take up the red sword, as Mother instructed. The haven of Anon Loam is nothing but a beautiful hiding place ruled by a treacherous queen.”

“A queen who made a deal to save her people,” I retorted before remembering I wasn’t supposed to have that knowledge.

Brianna stiffened and shook her head slightly. “You asked me what I want, and it is a life without hiding. I want the kingdom back, so I can rule if I choose or travel among the people if I wish it. I also want the angel of death and his armies gone. That is your purpose. That is what you were born to do. I shouldn’t have to beg you to fulfill your obligations to the crown.”

I stared at her, stunned by the coldness of her tone and the way she shaped her words. A thread of fear snaked through me, and I wondered what royal blood gave us. I sensed she was like Mother and would do whatever it took to get her way.

Suddenly, I didn't care about my nakedness. I stomped out of the pool, water slapping the stones as I reached for a towel. "Do you know who I am?" I hissed, wrapping the warmth around my body.

Brianna took a tiny half step back, as though I would hurl water at her.

"You're Evie Mor, firstborn, but only my half-sister."

Her gaze lingered on my bright red hair, and suddenly a bead of unease slowed me down. How much had Mother told her about me? I'd assumed the letter with the truth was private, something between Mother and me, but what if she'd told my siblings the truth? Suddenly, my insecurities flared up. The truth about who I was and my personal identity was wrapped up in my parents. Once I'd found my mother, I thought I'd have a purpose, and while she gave me direction, it wasn't what I expected.

"How do you know I'm only your half-sister?"

Brianna frowned. "It's obvious. You look just like our mother, but you have flaming red hair. She left you behind because she didn't want Father to know about you. Who you truly are. She was afraid."

I kept my reaction to myself. Mother was many things, but I doubted fear was the reason she'd given me up. The droplets of water on my bare skin left me shivering with cold, but I didn't want to dry myself off in front of my half-sister or let her see the bite mark on my side. I forced myself to speak, even though my lips trembled. "What was she afraid of? The kingdom was gone. She was on the run. Why be afraid of a child?"

Brianna's voice dropped to a harsh whisper. "You take me to be a fool? I wouldn't come to you unless I knew you could help. But you're selfish, aren't you? You're the child of a god. How many would wish for such power, such divinity, and you stand here, tossing it away because you weren't the one who got to grow up with your parents and siblings? Don't you know it's because Mother knew you were too good for us? You'd always be above, always better than us, and she was right. You can't even be bothered to help the kingdom of men because it doesn't fit into your personal needs. There's a reason no one believes in the old gods anymore or follows their ways. They let down the humans, and you're on your way to becoming just like them. I had hoped that the human side of you would see reason, but you're just like them, aren't you? Too good for this world. So go, figure out who you are, find your destiny, and leave us to our plight."

I stepped back as if she'd slapped me, my mouth

gaping as the truth of her words resonated. It was similar to what Takari had said, except this time it wasn't padded with love, but with the brutal truth. Expectations weighed heavy on my shoulders, and if I didn't step forward to fight, to take back the kingdom of men, the humans would loathe me. If they knew about Adomos, they'd hate me.

A storm of magic swirled in my belly, wanting to be unleashed upon Brianna, but it would only make everything worse. Breathing through my nose and exhaling with my mouth—like I'd learned in the Meditation Meadow—I took back control over my magic and emotions. "Your words are quite cutting, considering this is our first conversation."

Brianna lifted her chin. "You assume that you're the only one with magic, but you don't know about my skills or what I can do. I'm well aware that you are dangerous. You're a warrior, you can slay, but if you take up the red sword, you can kill him."

Him. Kedron Abbadon. My blood turned to ice in my veins.

"Think about what I've said," Brianna instructed, as though she were already queen. "The council will meet tomorrow. They will ask of you and you don't want them as your enemy. Think about what freedom means. You're a goddess, and you have the means to free us if you wish it."

Thoughts crashed through my mind. I wanted to light a ball of fire and hurl it at her just to frighten her. But threads of truth laced her words. “My father may be a god, but my mother was human,” I said.

“Don’t use that as an excuse,” Brianna scoffed.

At that moment, she sounded like Reish, and a slow, sneaking sensation came over me. What if Brianna had some kind of magic that gave her wisdom beyond her years? Now she appeared haughty, but the words she had spoken hit as though she’d punched me hard in the gut.

“Consider those who suffer,” Brianna continued. “Think about the children who were torn away from their families and raised by strangers who used and abused them. Think about those who grew up without love, without being cared for. Who will always search for a place to belong. Consider your actions and how you could free them from the angel of death who rules without regard for people. Hiding isn’t living. We shouldn’t be afraid to walk outside beyond the doors of our homes. Living is exploring. It is adventure, being able to have the freedom to choose. That’s what you want, isn’t it? The freedom to choose who you are, who you become, but no one has that choice when we live in bondage.”

“It’s been twenty years. What do you know of

bondage?" I demanded. If she kept talking, if she said more words that resonated, I would lose my control.

"I may have lived underground, but I have ears. I've heard the stories, the refugees searching for a place to call home, the villages attacked for sport, and the demons preying on the weak. Why do you think so many people lived underground with us? They weren't there because they loved the royal family. They were there for safety. A queen in hiding is still a queen as long as she continues her duties, and that's what Mother did. She took the people in and cared for them, made sure the trolls wouldn't bother us, and the elven queen's magic could protect us."

I stared at her, fighting with myself. "Why there though? Why not in Anon Loam or here in the Hall of Defenders, and what happened to the king?"

Brianna's eyes flashed, and she stepped back. "I didn't come here to have you pick apart decisions that were made before your time. I just came here to ask if you're willing to be like Mother and forsake your needs to help us. Once the angel of death is dead, you'll be free to go your own way. If you wish it. Think on those words. Sister."

She hurled the last word at me like a well-aimed dagger then hurried out of the cavern.

A whisper of confusion rose from the pool and I stared at it, a bleakness rising in my soul. The path before me was set. I didn't have a choice until I freed myself from my sure future.

9

After dressing, I trembled all the way back to the healing rooms, torn between indignation and rage and resignation. How dare my sister toss all those words at me with her prideful and haughty attitude? I wanted to go back and hurl a ball of fire at her, which was unlike me. Ever since I'd taken up the red sword, something within me had shifted, and now my hate and anger surfaced much faster than it used to.

My thoughts flickered back to Kedron Abbadon, and the bite on my side throbbed as though it were alive and sympathized with my plight. He hadn't killed me because he wanted me to change and become his queen. Because he knew the truth about me.

I wondered how many others knew. Brianna considered herself some kind of ruler, perhaps queen since Mother had died. Yet she hadn't told me what happened to the king. That must be important because she'd fled the moment I mentioned it. Still, she alluded to a kind of power she held, and I wasn't sure what to think about her. It was clear we'd never be friends because the tension between us was so fraught we could be enemies. My stomach soured at that idea, but all thoughts of her fled as I ducked into the darkened room where Romulus lay.

The young woman who'd led me there beckoned to Takari, who stood. "Evie, you're just in time. He woke up and asked for you."

My hands shook even more and a response would not leave my lips, so I forced my legs to move. I collapsed in the chair by Romulus's side, the candle casting enough light for me to see his face. It was deathly pale with sweat on his forehead, even though a bowl of cool water sat beside me with a towel. I assumed Takari had attempted to cool him down.

He lay as though asleep, and it was a few moments before his eyelids flickered and hazy gray eyes met mine. "Evie."

I leaned closer, disliking the dimness of his eyes. The hard ice that was gone from them. His fingers moved and on instinct, I took his warm hand in mine. It was something I never would have done before, but now the tension between us had faded. I wondered at what it had been at all. At first, I wanted him and dreamed he'd be the first one to kiss me, but after I met Adomos again, my feelings for him had shifted. I wondered if Romulus was angry at me for choosing Adomos over him, even though it wasn't for romantic reasons. A half-demon. That was the reason he was upset.

"I'm here, Romulus, but you should sleep. Try to get better."

He coughed and his chest rattled as though there was too much fluid inside. "They stabbed me deep and darkness filled my dreams. I'm not sure if I will, if I can, go on."

"It wasn't your fault." I squeezed his hand. "It was the angel of death and his elites. They are on the hunt and attacking anyone they find on the road."

"Did he tell you that?"

I stiffened. "If by he, you mean Adomos, no. I saw the dead with my own eyes and I. . ." I trailed off, unwilling to share my encounter with Kedron Abbadon.

"Will you fight back? With up the red sword? Take back the kingdom of men?" His words were heavy, each question followed by a pause and labored breathing.

I wrinkled my forehead. “It’s what everyone wants me to do, but I’m not sure. I remember when you first told me about the defenders, and how the kingdom of men was corrupt. Maybe it shouldn’t be a kingdom anymore. But the people are still cowed by what happened two decades ago, and the threat of the angel of death is real again. I don’t think my focus should be to restore the kingdom but to free the people.”

Romulus closed his eyes, and a slight smile came to his lips. When he spoke, it was slow but steady. “I hoped you’d come to that conclusion on your own, and I’m proud of you for taking up the red sword. It is dangerous, but you have magic and the blood of the gods. Surely you can overcome its lure. Evie, I always imagined you’d go back with me to Norbrin, to use the red sword to free the ice people from the rule of my mother.”

The finality of his words struck me and my jaw trembled as I spoke. “We’ll go. When you get better, I’ll go with you to the north.”

“Evie. I don’t think I’ll see the north again.”

He was trying to be kind, to let me know it was the end. Tears brimmed in my eyes and I shook my head. “Romulus, don’t talk like that. You’re a prince, a ranger, my friend. You can't give up and die. . .you. . ."

He interrupted. "Promise me you'll go, with or without me. Free the world, free the people, become the goddess the world needs."

"Romulus," I begged. "You're so young. You have so much life ahead of you."

A sad smile played about his lips as he closed his eyes. And then he went still.

"Romulus," I pleaded.

His hand around mine tightened for a few moments before it went limp, and I knew, even before his body went cold, that I was the only one breathing in that room.

I lay my head on his chest and wept.

10

Romulus' funeral was held the very next day. Instead of burying him, they placed him in a stone coffin and took him into the bowls of the mountain where he'd rest until the defenders could transport his body back to Norbrin. A numbness came over me as I watched the proceedings, and it all passed over me in a wave of silence, the tears I'd cried the night before frozen within. Who had Romulus been to me? One of my friends, that was for sure, and I was grateful we'd had a moment to make amends before he took his last breath. Still, I wondered about the ice people, the freedom they sought, and why Romulus believed in me and the red sword. Even Takari had expressed her disapproval of using such a weapon, sure that it would overpower me, and yet, I still hadn't heard the voice of the red sword since I'd met Kedron Abbadon.

"Evie." Takari sat down beside me, her eyes large and sad. "The council is waiting."

"They still want to meet?"

Takari signed and leaned her head against my shoulder. "Aye. There have been many deaths, and they want a plan of action. Romulus is not the only casualty in this war, although it feels like it since we are closest to him."

I closed my eyes and balled my hands into fists, reminded of the torn bodies I'd seen outside the cave, and the mutilated one on the road. The defenders would not pause their duty because of death, but I wanted nothing to do with them. A flame of anger burned in my belly and I recognized it as the need for vengeance. After my mother's death and Jezebel's torture, I'd felt that same thread of hatred, but back then, fear overrode all of it. This time, my hate was stronger than my fear.

Something clicked inside me as Takari stood and pulled me to my feet. I followed her down the dark passageways to the room where the council would meet. Inside, I considered what I would do. Part of me was human, but the other part of me was a goddess, powerful and immortal. I controlled the red sword and the fate of the kingdom of men.

As much as I hated to admit it, Brianna was right. The angel of death had to die, the people had to be free, and I was the one to do it. But if I took up such a task, it had to be on my own terms. I'd still go to find my father and try not to dwell on the fact that my identity was tied up with why he tricked my mother and who he wanted me to become. Instead of focusing on the past, I needed to ask for help and a strategic plan to take down the angel of death. Adomos was coming with me once I found him again.

"Evie, Takari, thank you for joining us." Nolani stood in the middle of the room and gestured to seats.

I glanced at the circle of people, young and old, women and men. Most of them were human who'd gathered. Instead of cheers and applause today, they looked at Takari and me out of somber eyes. I recalled that Romulus was one of their number, and it was likely their hearts were heavy with grief, too. I wasn't alone in this, nor did I see anyone looking at me as their savior. At least, not until I scanned the room and noticed Brianna and Solane. They weren't looking at me, but I noticed the way they held themselves, as though they were above all others. Had they entered the Hall of Defenders to be treated like royalty? My conversation with Brianna had certainly implied that.

Not wanting to think about their desires, I tucked my hands into my lap and shifted my gaze away from them. For once, it was a relief not to be the center of attention, nor have to request clemency from the elven queen.

Nolani waited just a moment as she stood in the middle of the circular room, all eyes on her. She turned, pivoting to look at each person before she spoke. Her words carried through the room, the solemnness haunting, "Today, we gathered to bury a friend, a comrade, one of our own whose life was taken far too early because of the blight of darkness that gathers in this land. Instead of today's meeting being a time to discuss, debate, and come up with a plan, we are in dire need. Too many of our friends have been cut down on their way home and bodies left mutilated in the wood. A new presence has entered our land, making it difficult to come and go as we used to. Our supplies are limited, and we need a solution."

She paused, perhaps for dramatic effect, but one man stood, his burly arms crossed and a thick beard hiding most of his face. "Why now? We've been here for years, unbothered, and the shadows in the wood have never come this close before. Scouts claim our cave of provisions has been discovered and taken over, and the only thing that has changed recently is the coming of the royals. Someone knows they are here and is coming to kill them."

I stiffened at the boldness of his speech and the audacity he had to blame it on my siblings. I willed myself to glance at them. If they accepted the burden of guilt, nothing displayed on their faces for they sat still, expressions blank. Determined to practice empathy, I put myself in Brianna's place and realized the oppression she lived under. Freedom. She couldn't run away like I could or fight back with weapons and magic. She had to sit in these halls using her wit until she was captured or freed. Her existence must be miserable. It was pity and anger that made me stand to my feet and address the man.

"You speak out in fear, but your blame is misplaced. It's not because of the royals, as you call us. My siblings came to these halls for safety. Would you toss them out after all they've been through? They've lived a life of hiding and fear; a life I've known nothing about. You know who I am, Evie Mor, princess of the kingdom of men."

With each word I spoke, my voice gained, growing louder and stronger and my confidence soared brought on by the edge of anger. "I did not want to come here. I was content to roam the world, searching for meaning and purpose. However, my friends, Romulus and Takari, asked me to take a chance and meet with the defenders before I continued on my quest. En route, we came upon a mutilated body in the woods and I went to investigate, leaving my friends in what I assumed was relative safety. I quickly learned that I was wrong. Your cave of provisions has been overrun. I went inside and discovered that none other than Kedron Abbadon and his elite warriors are the scourge that haunts this wood. They are out there killing because they want us to be afraid. They want us to live in fear and then give in to their demands and make a deal. But they made one fatal mistake; they killed my friend. Romulus. Prince of Norbrin. He is one of your own, and I'll tell you what I do to those who take from me. I take their lives with the red sword."

A gasp went through the room along with a wave of murmurs, but I raised my hands to quiet them down. "I'm not done yet either. You see, I grew up far from here in the Beluar Woods hidden away with the centaurs. I'd never met another human until I left the sacred forests in search of my mother. When I found her, the woman you knew as Queen Ceana, she was killed by the fallen goddess, Jezebel. I waited and bid my time by learning magic in Anon

Loam. When I left, I took the red sword with me, a weapon I'm sure many of you are familiar with, but unlike others, I will master it. In fact, I already have because I used it to kill Jezebel, and I tell you this. I will find Kedron Abbadon and I will slay him because his armies killed Romulus and took him away from us. I did not come here to ask for your help because I need assistance from the gods. So hold fast and stay firm in your fortress here. One day I will return victorious. In the meantime, I need a horse and provisions. I'm going to hunt."

They stared at me and when I stepped away from my seat someone else rose. "How do you know it is the angel of death and his elites?"

The truth was a fact I wanted to keep to myself, but instead, I lifted my chin. "I meet him; I fought his elites. It was him."

"Impossible. He would have killed you on sight!" Another man leaped up, shaking a finger.

I crossed my arms. "Do you know him? Personally? Can you guess his actions? Because he knew who I was and if I had to guess you don't know who I am."

Out of the corner of my eye, I saw Brianna flinch.

"You're Evie Mor, Princess of Labraid," someone said.

"True, but I am more, much more than just a

princess." I stepped into the middle of the room invading Nolani's space. "My father is not Conan Mor, but a god, which makes me a goddess. Which is why I have the power to free you from the angel of death."

11

A stunned silence filled the chamber with tension after my bold announcement. The truth was a fact I'd planned to keep to myself, especially after being captured and abused by Jezebel. Carrying the blood of the god was dangerous and led me to believe it would make to a target for others to take advantage of. After killing Jezebel, I knew it was a dangerous gift. I was imbued with more power and magic than I fully comprehended, which made me dangerous. It did not explain why the angel of death had not killed me, leaving me to assume, as an immortal, he wanted me for some dark purpose.

Nolani was the first to recover, and she

approached me tentatively, her eyes brimmed with tears. “So it is true, and you will do this?”

I crossed my arms, taken aback by her response. “I will,” I confirmed, wondering what rumors had been spread about me. Sure it hadn’t come from Brianna.

“We hoped, but we dared not ask. It is the motto of the defenders to allow you to use your free will to decide your fate. We need all the help we can get and our best fighters are those who volunteer,” Nolani explained. “Tell us, what can we do to help assist you? We are warriors and healers. We want to help.”

I raked my mind because I hadn’t expected this, her willingness to work alongside me and to put the defenders under my leadership. I recalled a time when someone had told me that I would be a leader. Now was too fast, too soon. I recalled the plan I’d come up with in the vale, and how proud I’d been to offer a solution to those people. What I didn’t know was the power of Jezebel and that she was coming for them. They’d all died and there was nothing I could do about it. But if I didn’t answer, I’d look weak in front of the assembly. Words tumbled out of my mouth. “It will take time for me to defeat the angel of death. In the meantime, you must survive. One of you mentioned supplies. How long will they last and how long until you need more?"

A woman in the back row stood up, speaking softly. "We have at least a month of supplies left. The trouble is the cave was our resource, and now it has been taken. We had supplies there waiting for transport, not only food for us, but for the horses, weapons to defend ourselves, and healing supplies. We are running low, and if we don't transport those goods within the month, we'll have to ration meals and those who fall ill may die."

I kept my fists tight for I had no desire to return to the cave, and yet if I wanted to help the defenders, I had to. I had fought one of the elites, though. And if I found Adomos and he helped, we might hold off the squad long enough to procure the goods. Moving them up the mountain would be slow and take more than a day. Suddenly, a weariness crept over me. It was all too much, and I wanted to leave and out in the wild again, hunting and fighting, what I was best at.

"I will find a solution," I addressed the woman. "For now, I must go, but I will return within the month."

As much as I despised taking on their burdens, it had to be done. I would not stand by while they starved. They were the first people who recognized who I was, yet set back and gave me a choice. Without waiting for a response, I spun on my heel and left the hall.

"Wait!" Someone called out.

"Let her go," another responded.

Relieved to be left alone, I stepped into the stone passageway and leaned against the wall. Closing my eyes, I lifted my face to where the sky should be, even though nothing but heavy rock rose above hemming me in. My chest felt tight and the small breaths of air I sucked in did nothing to quell my panic. The past twenty-four hours rushed into me, the facts glaring.

The angel of death was on the prowl.

Romulus was dead.

My siblings were in the Hall of Defenders.

And I'm promised to kill the angel of death to set everyone free.

But would it be enough? In the old songs and stories told in the sacred forests, the seasons of life changed and yet rotated in similar cycles. Each year, the four seasons included spring, summer, fall, and winter, so the cycles of the land of Labraid stayed the same. The powerful oppress the weak, a hero rises to strike back and bring peace, but only for a time until another dark power grew, worse than the last. And so the cycle continued.

If I took down the angel of death, who would rule in his place?

I sensed a presence and knew I wasn't alone anymore. I opened my eyes, halfway expecting to see Reish since she had a tendency to appear when I was in need. Instead, it was Brianna, yet again. I glared at her. She was the last person I wanted to see. In my current state of mind, it would be near impossible to keep my temper in check.

"I came to say thank you," she announced.

Her tone implied she wasn't grateful, but sensed I was doing my duty and that annoyed me. "I have done nothing yet," I retorted.

"No, but you made a choice and gave us hope. Don't underestimate the power of hope. When you came to our underground hiding place, you brought hope with you, but that goddess quickly tore it away when she attacked. We didn't know if you were living or dead, and eventually, we heard word that Mother had been slain, but your body hadn't been found. Now you're here, and I sense it is only the beginning. I came to tell you; I'm your ally. We might have the same mother, and we might be royals, but I don't want us to be corrupt or carry bad blood between us." She extended her hand. "I don't know if we'll ever be friends, but I hope we can come to a truce."

Not friends, but allies. That fate resonated with me because, truthfully, I wasn't sure what I wanted from my sister if anything at all. The rift of not growing up together was too wide, and she had a keen sense of my bitterness toward her, although it was no fault of her own. I stuck out my hand and met hers. When our skin touched, a tingling sensation brushed up my arm, making it numb and itchy. My training with the elves had taught me to recognize magic, and it was there hovering just under the surface.

I stared at her, eyes wide. "You have magic."

She snatched her hand away and hugged it to her chest as though she could hide what I'd felt.

"It's not odd to have magic," she asserted.

"No, I just. . ."

"You assumed," She cut me off, not unkindly though. "Mother had magic, too. You probably inherited some of hers, but she'd mastered the ability to hide it."

I stared at Brianna openly. Perhaps I'd misjudged her. "She never told me," I admitted. Thinking back, all of our conversations had been about me, my past, and my future. The brief conversations we'd had centered on my needs and my anger, and in my drive to understand why she'd forsaken me. I hadn't gotten to know her.

"No, she didn't like to talk about herself."

Brianna stared at the wall, and I detected loss and sorrow in the way she held herself. I wasn't the only one who had suffered during the attack and while I was subject to physical torture, perhaps Brianna had suffered under the mental torture of finding herself alone and in charge of her younger siblings. A softness swelled, and I wanted to tell her I understood, but she pulled herself together quickly. The moment of sorrow passed, replaced by hardness as she gave herself a shake. "Anyway, I thought you should know. I have no hard feelings towards you, despite our conversation yesterday."

I opened my mouth to respond when the doors swung wide and people began filing out. The council was over.

12

My horse nuzzled my shoulder as if he'd missed me. Taking the reins, I rubbed his nose, admiring the sheen of his clean coat. He'd been brushed and well-fed in the past day. Now he was saddled and carried a pack of supplies on his back. As for myself, I wore a new pair of clothes, including a shirt, long trousers, and a cloak for warmth and obscurity. The red sword was strapped to my back and determination surged within.

Takari appeared as I swung up and touched my leg. "You won't stay another night, will you? Set off when it's light?"

She was right. It would be best to wait, but if I spent another moment in the fortress, I'd scream.

"No, I'm going to hunt and find Adomos. I'll be fine, but what about you?"

She shrugged, blinking away tears. "I'll stay here, for now. Eventually, I continue my search or return to the elves."

This was goodbye. I pressed a hand to my heart and held her gaze. "I wish you well."

"The same to you, Evie."

I sensed more unsaid words floating on her tongue, but she did not speak again, only squeezed my leg.

Tearing my gaze away, I clucked to the horse who walked to the exit of the barn while the guards opened the doors to let me through. Eion was among them and he saluted me, bringing a half-smile to my lips.

I trotted into the tunnel and moments later I was free, the tang of pine on my tongue as I bent low over the horse's back encouraging it to gallop into the wood. A rush of emotion shivered through me as the wind whipped by, tugging at the cloak, treads of coolness threatening to numb me. Oh, I wanted the wind and the intense chill. I wanted my fingers to tingle from pain and take away the black hole that swelled inside my heart. If only I'd listened. If only I'd joined the defenders earlier, could Romulus' death have been avoided?

Lost in grief, I gasped when a flock of crows rose from a tree, cawing as they flew away. Heart thudding, I yanked on the reins bringing the horse to a stop. The daylight had slid away while I rode, and the enormous trees towered above me. Cold sweat dripped down my back and I took a deep breath considering whether it was wise or foolish of me to run away. I needed to rest and make camp while there was still lingering light, but part of me wanted to press on and lose myself on the winding track. If the elites were out there, if HE were out there, I wanted to fight, to hurt, to bring pain, and to make them feel the way I felt.

What did I have to lose? I needed to go back to the cave and transport the supplies back to the Hall of Defenders. I dismounted, suddenly weary at the very idea and questioning why I'd considered myself brave enough to come to their aid. Even with Adomos, I could not imagine how one horse could help transport their supplies back to them. It would have been wise to ask for help, or at the very least, instead of fleeing, stay and plan with them.

But I had fled.

My fingers tingled as an impulsive idea strayed into my mind. Without weighing the cost, I flung off the cloak and pulled the red sword free.

It was quiet in my hands, and I wondered if

Kedron Abbadon had done something to it with his peculiar magic. Wrapping both hands around the hilt, I held on and waited. It came slowly, a vibration like a heartbeat. A pulse of red flickered and then it rushed through me like a broken dam. A flood of desire for blood and death and darkness.

I stepped away from the horse following the tug of destruction deeper into the wood. The light around me faded faster than expected. Daylight sinking into the shaded shadows of eve. Lightning bugs flickered showing me the way. Almost as though a host of lights were guiding me deeper. A high-pitched tinkling came like that of sweet bells except words were layered into the harmonies. Words I'd understand if only the voices spoke louder.

A sense of wonder filled me as though I were floating on the edges of reason. I followed the yellow lights down a hill toward the roots of a magnificent tree layered with dark green leaves and gray moss. The lights hovered around it creating a design, a word. Right before my eyes, the tree split open.

Golden light streamed out of it, blinding me. I shielded my eyes, mouth agape, sure I had ingested nothing that would cause the hallucinations. The sense of awe remained as the tree bathed me in light. Sweet voices sang in harmony as the light faded enough for me to see inside the tree. A miniature woman only three feet tall sat cross-legged on a speckled mushroom clothed in leaves as green as a sweet summer day. A crown of white flowers graced her golden head, and she pointed her scepter at me then stood.

The translucent wings on her back fluttered and her pointed ears perked up. I swallowed hard, taken aback because I'd seen creatures like these before, although ones much smaller than her. Fairies. Once, Romulus had saved me from being teased by the fey folk, and he knew their language. I had studied the languages of elves and fairies in Anon Loam, and while I was fluent in reading it, I hadn't become fluent in speaking it.

"Are you the one they call Evie Mor?" the fairy asked, her voice as sweet as syrup and so high the chirping of it pierced my ears.

"I am," I confirmed. What was the point of lying? She appeared to know who I was as though she were expecting me.

"Good," she said in her shrill voice waving her wand. A rainbow of pixie dust floated off it and sparkled on top of the mushroom. "I have a task for you."

A task, as though she had the right to control my

actions. My grip on the red sword tightened, but I braced myself to listen.

"I am the queen of the faerie, and this tree is home to my people. Lately, though, our wood has been filled with trespassers and the scent of death is stronger than the fragrance of flowers. It is a terrible inconvenience, but you can help rid us of those dark shadows destroying our wood and return the forest to the way it was before. We've heard about you, you know; the half-human who carries the red sword and killed a goddess. Shame, you killed her, but since only a god can kill a god, you must take her place as our protector."

The bark of a sharp laugh rose in my throat, and I almost spit it out, my body shaking with indignation. Me take the place of Jezebel? How absurd! Had Jezebel made a deal with the faeries and why would she agree to protect them? What did she get out of the deal? As if guessing my thoughts, the queen continued.

"Once you have freed our forest, we, of course, will be in your debt. I propose this. Since you came from the mountain where the humans dwell, we shall do you a favor and deliver their supplies to them."

This would solve my problem as well. My jaw tightened as I considered. I'd intended to fight the elite warriors haunting the wood anyway. But if the fairies would deliver the supplies, I could continue on my quest to find my father and plan a way to defeat Kedron Abbadon. Either way, we'd both get what we wanted and I could see no trickery in her proposal. "I accept," I announced.

"Marvelous!" the queen squeaked sending another rainbow of fairy dust dancing.

I wrinkled my nose and let out a violent sneeze, closing my eyes for just a moment. When I opened them, she waved a scroll and quill. "Sign here," she instructed.

Just the slightest inkling of doubt plagued me. "Why?"

She waved her hand as though bored. "It's just a formality, a quick agreement, nothing more."

Feeling woozy from the dust, I nodded and reached for the miniature quill. I had to squint to see the tiny words, all written out on the scroll. Briefly, I wondered where she obtained the quill and ink from so quickly, but I signed my name with a flourish and stepped back, all the while holding the sword.

The faerie queen straightened up, a smug look crossing her face. "Our deal starts now. I hope you can keep your end of the bargain. If not, there will be consequences."

It was only as the light from the tree faded as it closed that I recalled the words that Romulus had used. Fairies were mischievous and enjoyed their fun. But it was too soon to tell if I'd been pranked or if they would fulfill their end of the deal if I kept to the terms of the deal. What had possessed me to sign the silly contract?

Alone in the dark, a blanket of shadows enveloped, and a sudden sense of weariness made me want to curl up somewhere warm and sleep. I hadn't slept well the evening before, tossing and turning with too many thoughts and worries. Even meditating hadn't calmed me down, and I missed the serenity I'd gained in the Meditation Meadows.

My imagination envisioned shadows and skeletons as though I'd stepped into a crypt of bones. An eerie howl cut through the silence, setting my nerves on edge. At times in the Beluar Woods, the howl of a wolf pack would drift through the night as they hunted; never staying long for they knew the land belonged to the centaurs.

As the howl came again but it did not quite sound like a wolf but layered with a voice deeper and unearthly. The voice of something demonic. I spun around in the dark, cognizant that I was lost in the wood, unsure how to retrace my steps back to the horse.

"Adomos," I whispered wishing he were by my side.

Suddenly, a thread of hate coursed through my veins and the voice of the sword pulsed through me. The sword had re-awakened, and a thirst filled me. *Kill. Kill. Kill.*

13

This time, I didn't block it for if the elite warriors prowled in the dark then the sword would lead me to them. The sword sang, and I took a step. My footsteps were steady as I moved toward the eerie sounds of the night. Bushes rustled and the wind chasing through the trees sounded like the cry of a wraith calling for those who were lost. Cold sweat dried on my neck as I moved deeper following the cry of the sword. Blood roared through my ears and the bite mark on my side itched, as though it, too, was driven by the need to destroy.

The whoosh of an arrow made me duck behind a tree, and just in time, it smacked into the trunk with tiny pieces of wood flying. Was it possible that my enemy could see in the dark? I suddenly needed to set us on even footing and hurled a ball of fire into the thicket. Squatting at the foot of the tree trunk, I watched it arc lighting up the forest ever so briefly and yet displaying none of the shadow warriors. A curse came to my lips, one the centaurs would be ashamed to hear me utter. But I was done with those cares and worries.

Life had not been kind to me after leaving the sacred woods, and I wondered if the gods even cared if any practice the old ways or if they had forsaken Labraid to its demons.

Another arrow whistled past me, and as a shape materialized out of the darkness. In hurling the ball of fire, I'd given away my cover. Stepping back, I aimed and sent a ball of fire into the chest of my assailant. Even though he was armored, he staggered back, and I lunged with the red sword striking true. The sword hissed against armor and an unearthly glow came out of it. Red smoke billowed into the air and the acid scent of burning stung my nostrils.

Kill. Kill. Kill.

The voice buzzed all around me, filling my senses. It didn't seem wrong to reach out and slay these elite warriors, monsters that might be half-demon. The armies of the angel of death had taken so much from me. The truth stung as I pulled back my arm and whipped my sword around to slice at the warrior sneaking up on me. Raw edges of a blade sliced through my skin and I hissed but did not stumble. Summoning my magic, I hurled a ball of fire, ducked from another blow, and drove the sword up into the warrior's torso.

He staggered, but before he hit the ground another shadow warrior took his place. The sword's voice roared in my ears and I raised it, only to be blocked by an ax. The impact was so hard my shoulder jarred. Grinding my teeth, I kicked out, swung my sword around, and looped off the head of the warrior.

Kedron Abbadon and his armies had taken everything from me. That thought rang clearly as more warriors poured out of the wood, two or three at a time, and I fought with blade and magic.

If not for him, I would have grown up with a mother and father. A proper princess of the kingdom of men imbued with magic and strength and power. I would have gotten to know my siblings. We might have been friends if the past had changed. Romulus wouldn't be dead. Takari might not have lost her mate. The elves wouldn't have been forced to make a deal with Kedron Abbadon and all would have been well.

I slashed and ducked, weaved and cleaved, as the

dark thoughts swirled through my mind in a melody of madness. It was his fault that I was here, forced to fight back, to take the kingdom of men back, to save the defenders, and to free my siblings. He was the reason for everything and if I destroyed the grip he had on Labraid and claimed it for the royal family, I would have vengeance.

Blades flashed and fire burned, and at last a sea of blood and burned bodies lay around me, and the voice of the sword was silent. My arms trembled from sheer exhaustion and the well of magic deep inside was empty at last. I didn't see the sword drink in blood and ash, sated at last, but I felt its lust for death and destruction fade.

I weaved in place, my vision suddenly dizzy as I fell as though I were one of the dead too. A sudden light shone around me blinding in its pure white brilliance, and I let go of my grief and anger. All I wanted was to sleep and let this existence fade.

A sea of high-pitched voices chattered in a nonsensical language. Someone or something lifted me up and bore me away, and I wondered if the defenders had followed me after all and found me among the dead. Soon I'd be back in their solemn walls, and I could sleep away this madness. For I'd fallen victim to the voice of the sword and allowed it to control me.

FEATHER SOFT WHISPERS awoke me and a blinding headache throbbed in my skull so fresh and tender it was difficult to remember all that had happened. Without bothering to open my eyes, I used my other senses to discover what was around me. Moss under my fingers and something against my throat, my shoulders, waist, knees and ankles holding me down. I strained to lift my arms, but they were held fast, tied down by something that wasn't malleable. The sudden sensation of familiarity crept over me.

My heart sank as I forced myself to acknowledge the truth. I'd been taken prisoner. Again. Why and by whom was insignificant, I had to escape quickly. I summoned my magic, waiting for the warmth to bubble up within, but it did not come. It should have been easy, a spark on my fingertip to burn through the bonds and gain freedom. But a hollowness left my body empty and sore, and the headache would not go away.

Screwing up my face against the pain, I slowly forced my eyes open. Sloping rust-brown walls rose around me and I blinked as my eyes adjusted to the dim light. I was underground or in a cave, but a beam of soft light filtered in from somewhere behind me. I tilted my head back to look and my head throbbed as if I'd been stabbed. Suppressing a cry, I closed my eyes again, forcing myself to stay calm. I'd figure a way out of this situation.

I strained again my bonds again, but they held me fast almost as though someone with magic had captured me. But who had magic more powerful than my own? The arrogant thought passed through my mind along with the knowledge that after learning magic and taking the red sword, I considered myself invincible against all. Who was more powerful than the gods? I refused to believe yet another god had captured me. Maybe I was in Kedron Abbadon's dungeon, but the way he treated me when we first met did not make me think he'd treat me like a prisoner.

A clinking sound made me perk up my ears. I kept my eyes closed as the sound came closer, and then a high-pitched and slightly familiar voice said, "It's all there, as promised."

"Clever queen, how did you get her to sign away her rights?"

"It's a secret I'll never tell. You have what you want, and I have what I want. One more thing." There came the sound of papers being shuffled. "She'll want proof. Show her this letter."

"As though that would make her compliant."

"I don't envy your dilemma, but you asked for this. Our business is done?"

"The money is all here. I look forward to working with you again in the future."

The shrill voice tittered with flirtatious laughter. "Don't be so sure it will happen again."

Their low voices carried away while I raked my mind for knowledge of who had laughed in such a way. Dread dawned on me as I considered my grief-stricken night, the odd meeting with the queen of the faerie, and the way I had allowed the sword to control me.

I'd signed on the scroll without fully reading it, but we'd made a deal. What if she'd double-crossed me? I recalled my first encounter with the fey folk, and how Romulus told me they enjoyed being mischievous. But we made a deal, or had we?

A sinking sensation stirred in my belly as I examined the room again. Low ceilings, the sound of dripping water, footsteps echoing above me, and myself tied down to a pallet. I turned my head toward the light and caught the glint of bars and the truth sank with a shock as though I'd fallen into icy waters.

I was locked in a prison cell.

14

The eerie scraping of a grate being pulled stung my ears, and the scent of a deep musk invaded my scenes as heavy footsteps clopped into the room. I swiveled my head around as a bulky shadow invaded my space, and I shrank back from the creature that stared down at me. My bonds were tight and it was useless, but I still struggled to put distance between myself and the creature. He had pale yellow reptilian eyes with narrow slits that blinked at me. While his head was human-like, his skin was a collection of multi-colored scales like a snake or lizards. His forked tongue shot out of his mouth as he licked his thin lips, eyeing me as though I were a tasty morsel to eat. When he rubbed his hands, sharp claws clattered together.

"What do you want with me?" I croaked out.

The lizard man grinned, his tongue flickering in and out of his mouth. "I just bought you from the faeries," he boasted shifting from foot to foot.

I narrowed my eyes. Those treacherous little beings. If only I were free, I'd burn their forest to the ground. The violence of my thoughts gave me pause. Surely I wasn't that vindictive. "I overhead you and the faerie queen talking, but we had a deal."

"Yes, yes." The lizard man giggled as if the entire situation was an elaborate joke and pulled a scroll out of his robes. "She said you'd want to see this."

He held it up, close enough so I could read it, but keeping his fingers far enough away so that I couldn't lean forward and bite him. Pity. I wanted to hurt him and again I wondered where that thought came from. That desire to hurt others and cause destruction. That wasn't how I usually felt about others, and even during the times I'd been at a disadvantage, I'd sought to find even ground with others.

Now, all I wanted to do was lash out, and I wondered if the red sword influenced me. Perhaps I'd listened to it too long last night. Pushing the thought away, I squinted in the low light, making out the words. It was a letter from Takari, of all people. I gasped.

Dear Evie - I hope you are well and understand you continued on your quest to find your father. We cannot thank you enough for making a deal with the fey folk to deliver the supplies. Besides your help, the scouts report the roads are clear and they have seen none of the warriors in the wood. We are still being careful and I hope to hear from you when you have gained a sense of direction for what to do next. I know the fey folk said you didn't want to return here, and that's fair. I understand that. Please understand we are grateful for your help and are here to assist if you would call upon us in the future. I know not where my road will take me, but I will tarry here a while longer before making any decisions. Go with grace and the blessing of the gods - Takari.

So the fey folk had kept their end of the bargain and still delivered me to this lizard man. But something about the letter felt off. "How long have I been here?"

"Since this morning. It took the faeries a week to deliver you. They said you were in some magical coma and apparently you're quite heavy to move. For them, at least. This is my first chance getting a good look at you and my, my, you're definitely worth the price." He reached out with his claws, lifting the end of my braid and unraveling it with his fingers.

"Take your hands off me," I hissed.

He snorted. "I'm the one giving orders now."

I tried again. "Do you know who I am?"

The lizard man attempted to roll his eyes but ended up shifting them back and forth awkwardly while he threw up his hands. "Evie Mor, the legendary lost princess, that's why we paid so much for you. Also found carrying the ancient red sword and rumored to have the blood of the gods. Word is, you killed the goddess, Jezebel." Shifting his eyes again, he lowered his voice in admiration. "Is that true?"

I barred my teeth at him, and a little growl escaped my throat. "Let me go."

Frowning, he stepped back. "I think not, and I'm a little insulted you didn't ask me to introduce myself, nor did you demand to know where you're at. As a prisoner, I expect your brain is slightly muddled, so I'll forgive those indiscretions this once."

I frowned right back at him, which caused another wave of pain to pierce my head and a hollowness in my stomach ate at me. Seven days, he'd said, without food or water, which explained the weakness. And my ancestry explained why I was still alive. I waited for him to explain, and he did not hesitate.

"You are in the underground prisons of Lizdarian, home of the lizard people. I am the Chief

Collector here and specialize in collecting dangerous and magical beings. We are proud to remove them from being a hindrance in Labriad and offer them a new life as gladiators of Lizdarian. You are the newest addition, and just before you came, we captured one of those legendary Nephilim."

My heart beat faster. Adomos? "Does he have blue skin and gold runes on his body?"

"How did you know?" the Chief Collector clapped his hands quite delighted.

"I've come across him in the past," I said carefully.

"Good, good. Well, you won't be seeing much of each other, at least not yet, but it would be delightful to schedule a fight between you."

I paused, suddenly aware of the strange word he used, gladiator. I hadn't heard it before, nor of the Lizdarians. "What is a gladiator?" I interrupted, cutting off his flow of words midstream.

He choked. "It's a fight, of course, between two mighty warriors."

The pounding in my head increased from a dull throb to a roar.

"You'll need to be cleansed, of course, and put on display for the audience. They do delight in seeing the dangerous magical creatures we've selected for their enjoyment. I'll have food and water brought, and the attendants will serve you. I have an outfit in mind for you. The audience will love your beauty. We'll have a replica made of your sword so you can look fearsome. It would give you an unfair advantage to use Claíomh Dearg. Keep in mind, all of our warriors have been deprived of magic to make the fight even, but I hear you barely need magic for a one-on-one contest, as this shall be. You'll bring in a lot of coin for us, and we will set aside some of it for you, should you last through the first round."

My vision tunneled as my mind whirled. The Chief Collector continued to babble, but his words became indistinguishable as I tuned him out. I'd left the Hall of Defenders to save the people from the angel of death. Instead, I'd made a misguided deal with the queen of faerie and now I was a warrior for sport.

15

The attendants weren't afraid of me. Even when I struggled and growled, they only scuttled away from me shrieking and giggling. They weren't fairies but reminded me of the fey folk with enormous eyes, tiny wings, and a height of only three feet tall. Their scaly skin glowed as though embedded with some kind of dust or the shards of a magical jewel.

When the attendants got over their initial shyness, they swarmed around me chatting excitedly in their own tongue. They expressed their words by waving hands and flitting their wings back and forth. The heavy fragrance of flowers that surrounded them made my headache worse. My limbs were falling asleep from being tied in one position for so long, and a powerful thirst made me lightheaded.

"Water," I croaked.

One screamed and pointed at my mouth, then dashed off and returned with a water jug. She set it by the foot of the bed and maneuvered something long, thin, and reed-like into the jar and guided it to my mouth. It took me a moment to realize she expected me to suck. I did and fresh, cool water flooded my mouth. I drank deeply, and strength surged through my body again. Yet a hollowness still lingered, perhaps from lack of food or the binding of my magic. What had the Chief Collector said about magic?

My thoughts scattered as the tiny creatures ripped off my clothes, using a combination of knife and teeth. I struggled. "Wait. Stop!"

They giggled ignoring my command even though I surmised they could understand me. I growled deep in my throat wishing I had magic that would spew out of my mouth like a fire-breathing beast and drive the pesky creatures away. They did not relent leaving me with one course of action.

Centering my focus, I pulled at my bonds, concentrating on the vines around my arms and legs I pulled as hard as I could.

A tearing sound came; followed by a volley of screams as I sat up. While I hadn't broken the bonds, I'd loosened them. With another tug, I might break them and be able to escape. The attendants buzzed around me. Their high-pitched shrieks were making me want to fling them across the room. Trying it ignore them, I studied my prison cell again. It was dingy with an iron grate for a door. I had to get past it if I hoped to escape.

Summoning my strength, I yanked on the bonds again and a fury of fire slammed into my back. Arching back, I squealed both from the shock of it and the burning sensation against my bare flesh.

"What is the meaning of this?" a deep voice bellowed.

I gasped for air while the heat in my back intensified. Scraps of clothing fell from my body, but there was nothing I could do to prevent the attendants from shredding the rest of my clothing. Meanwhile, the thud of hooves pulled my gaze toward the deep voice. It was a faun, with short horns in his curly hair, a whip in hand, and a muscled chest much like Adomos. He was at least six and a half feet tall, with a gold ring in his nose, and a scarred face set in a permanent scowl. He cracked the whip again, and I went still reminded of Jezebel.

One hand circled my throat as he yanked me

forward to face him. I squirmed under his grip unable to free myself and hating that I was helpless once again. Unlike the Chief Collector, he didn't display any giddy excitement, and I guessed he was tasked with keeping the gladiators in check.

"You might be the bastard princess of the kingdom of men, but here, you're nothing more than entertainment. I suggest you behave and prepare to contend. It will be your only chance at escape, and if you don't, I intend to make your life hell. I don't care where you came from or who you are; you're in my domain now."

His gaze slithered down my body, but instead of a lust-driven leer, he stared at me as though assessing a beast to purchase. His grip on my throat kept me from speaking, but his eyes darkened as he scrutinized me. With one violent shove, he slammed me flat against the bed.

I gasped for air as he held me down and the attendants cowered out of sight. Their quiet whimpers were the only sound that indicated they were still in the prison cell. Pressing the butt of the whip against my cheek, the faun pulled shreds of clothing away from my waist and ran his hand over my belly. As intimate as the caress was, I knew he did not mean it when he stopped and pinched my skin.

"By the gods, where did you get this mark?"

Rough fingers prodded tender skin and my face burned as he touched the only reminder I had of my encounter with the angel of death. The only way I knew what had happened wasn't a nightmare.

The pressure on my throat lessened as he moved his hand and barked out. "Tell me, where did you get this mark?"

I glanced down at my bare body, tilting my head at an awkward angle to see what he could see. A black mark stained my side, slowly spreading like jagged fingers of lightning. My eyes darted back to the fauns in alarm. "I. . . I don't know," I sputtered. "I was in the wood, fighting elite warriors, and then the faerie betrayed and sold me here."

"Tell me the truth," he snapped. "This is no ordinary mark. It's the signature of the devil."

And how would he know that?

But the faun wasn't done with me. "The devil defiled you, didn't he? Do you carry his spawn?"

He glared down my naked body with such hatred that I struggled to recoil. "Let me go," I begged. "I'm not a gladiator and never will be, and there are devilish creatures looking for me. It would be better for both of us if you just let me go."

A flash of teeth warned me of my error and the whip hissed out catching me across my chest. I squirmed to escape with the lash punishing but not hard enough to slice through skin. At least, not yet.

"You'd like that, wouldn't you," the faun growled. "You want to get me into trouble to save your own skin? The Chief Collector will not take kindly to this news, and I'll have the truth out of you if it's the last thing I do."

The whip sang out again harder this time, and I jolted back powerless unless I used my tongue. "It was the angel of death!" I cried out, hating myself for blabbing, yet seeing no way out of my situation.

The faun did not stop, though. His lashes came quicker, harder, crisscrossing my chest, shoulders, and stomach. Setting my teeth, I clenched my legs together, the only action I could take to protect myself.

When the whip cracked over my nipples, I cried out with heat and blood rising. When at last the faun stopped, I lay still. Chest heaving. My body was riddled with marks. "Goddess indeed," he spat and stepped back.

The pain faded as he ceased replaced with fury. It boiled through me like hot lava. Gritting my teeth, I yanked on my bonds which came loose with a snap.

The faun stepped back eyes flashing as he eyed the chains on my arms and legs. But I was free enough. I sprang to my feet as the attendants wailed and scurried away shouting about a prisoner escaping. Let them come. The faun had stroked my ire, and even my nakedness could not stop me from taking action. I had to beat him down, find Adomos, and escape.

He grinned as I lifted my hands. "You forgot one thing. Magic doesn't work here. You'll have to use your brute strength."

I had forgotten, but I folded my hands into fists and sprang at him. He ducked away with surprising speed, and I lifted my knee kicking out at his groin. I missed, which set me off balance and he circled me coiling the whip with his fingers. Then, as if coming to a decision, he tossed it away.

I eyed the whip, knowing my skills were with either magic or blade. My daggers were practical in overcoming those larger than me, and he was much bigger with hooves that would punish me if I didn't watch out. I punched at his face. He returned with a blow to my stomach. I bent over at the waist, gasping for breath as his elbow slammed into my back knocking me flat on the ground. I rolled out of reach and with a kick knocked his hooves out from under him. He went down hard, but I howled with pain as my bones hurt from the impact of kicking him.

Quick to recover, I rose to my knees and

punched him hard in the face. He merely grunted and drove his fist into my mouth. The coppery tang of warm blood filled my mouth and dribbled down my chin. Clenching my jaw, I threw another blow only for it to be blocked by his arms. He rolled, taking me with him, and in a tangle of limbs, we struggled on the ground with rock digging into my back as he pushed me down. He drove a fist directly into my bite mark. I cried out as a burst of heat flared, making my stomach cramp.

Suddenly, his hand was around my neck, and even though I bucked and kicked, he held me down. "This is why magic is not useful here," he said, smug. "Brute violence is your only strength, and if you want to win in the area, you need to be stronger. In a fight to the death, you'd be dead already. I'm supposed to be your trainer. To help you get stronger and become a powerful contender, but now, knowing the angel of death has marked you, I want nothing to do with you."

"Why?" I gasped for air, my fingers around his wrists, digging into his skin as I tried to free myself from his grasp.

"Because if the angel of death has marked you, it means you're his and he will come for you. Mark my words."

I glared at him, trying to let him see my hate, but

he continued to hold me down and apply pressure to my throat. My vision went dizzy at first, my chest constricted as I struggled and clawed at his solid arm. My movements turned frantic as I faded into blackness.

16

When the attendants returned, I did not protest as they bathed and dressed me in what they called clothing and what I called rags. They wrapped cloth around my chest, so tight it was difficult to breathe and left my navel and waist bare. To add insult to injury, they tied a skirt around my waist. It sat low on my hips and fell to my knees, with a split up both sides, almost to my waist. It almost would have been better to be naked than to be exposed in such a shameful way.

They brushed my flaming red hair until it shone, but instead of braiding it, they left a wave of curls cascading down my back, a false curtain of modesty. The faun returned to chain my hands in front of me and connected the chain to the shackles around my feet. Unable to lift my hands more than a few inches, it was impossible for me to remove the gag he'd shoved into my mouth. Finally, it put a collar around my neck and fastened it to a leash. Clasped in irons so tight I could barely move, I shuffled after him out of the cell. Many words came to mind as I followed him down the passageway, but muffled threats were the only sound that came out of my throat.

Days ago, I'd been ungrateful about my position in life, even though I was on my way to the Hall of Defenders and traveling with friends. Now, I was hidden in some prison that blocked magic, being led by a grumpy faun who wanted to get rid of me. How far I'd fallen from grace. Would I always be this unlucky in life? Trying not to feel sorry for myself, I focused on my surroundings.

The faun led me up a flight of stairs, and in the distance, sounds of grunts and the smack of flesh against flesh echoed. A hint of iron hung in the air. Blood, I guessed, although the gag blocked my airway and made it difficult to breathe and smell. The howl of a beast sent shivers up my spine, but we moved higher where daylight crept in. The light was brilliant and beautiful. I'd missed the warm glow of sunlight, the sweet smell of morning dew, and the soft strains of harp music in Anon Loam. I'd grown antsy in the peaceful haven, and my impulsive decision had led to all this. A lump swelled in my throat. I had to escape, sooner rather than later, and take Adomos with me. As my eyes darted around the cavernous prison, no obvious escape routes appeared. My spirits sank lower at the idea of fleeing without using magic.

Over the past year, I'd grown comfortable with my newfound magic, using it as a crutch to defend myself. My lack of knowledge regarding magic was the reason Jezebel had found, captured, and tortured me. A dark thought pushed at the edges of my mind because it was my fault my mother was dead. I'd given away her location because I didn't know how to hide my magic, and it had shone like a beacon inviting Jezebel to find me.

Now I used magic as a shield to prevent the cruel claws of the world from reaching me. Except, I'd failed and even my skill with the blade could not save me. Blades. My chest went tight as I considered what had happened to the red sword. All my senses told me I needed it to defeat the angel of death. Being part goddess hadn't given me an advantage in the past, and I did not expect one in the future. However, the Lizdarians had taken it from me, and I needed to find it before I escaped.

At last, the faun halted and rapped twice on a

door. It swung open; the doorway flanked by guards. We entered a daylight-filled room and my eyes widened unsure of what to look at first. The open space was an enormous covered balcony with low gray couches along the wall, and a set of three wide stairs leading up to a third-tier near the railing. Before me stretched a golden table, sagging under the weight of exotic foods, wines, and an entire pig with steam rising off it. The tang of oranges and a dark wine hung in the air along with a hint of mint from the vines growing down the roof. The sight of all that food made my mouth water, and the gag forced a pool of drool to dribble out of my mouth. Sloppy, but with my hands bound, I was powerless to wipe my mouth.

On one side of the steps stood a group of musicians and half-dressed dancers swayed their hips seductively to the low music that played in the background. I turned my eyes away, my face flushing from their lack of clothes, wondering if I, too, looked like a sinful offering about to be given to the one who'd purchased me. Thinking of the Chief Collector, my eyes darted around the room full of people. Only a few of them were human. Most of them were Lizdarian, and none of them gave the faun and me much attention. Other than a brief look, they returned to what they had been doing before we entered, eating, drinking, or discussing. A few of them pulled dancers into their laps or stroked their legs inappropriately.

At last, I located the Chief Collector on the top tier beside the railing. A small table had been placed there, and he was one of the two who sat around it staring down at the view, which I could not see. When his reptilian gaze met mine, he clasped his hands together and motioned to his companion. My heart beat faster as his companion—another Lizdarian—turned. He was radiant, with dark eyes and scales that shone like gold making it difficult to focus on him but impossible to look away. Black hair was slicked down his skull, and he waved his clawed hands welcoming us to approach.

When he stood, robes swept the ground, and the faun yanked at my leash. I moved as quickly as I could, not wishing to fall on the steps.

"What had you brought us, Ohran?" The Chief Collector grinned, clinking his claws together.

I glanced at the faun whose forehead creased as though he didn't like being called by his first name. "It's Master Ohran to you, Chief Collector," he retorted, then bowed his head to the golden-scaled man. "Your eminence, we have a problem."

The Chief Collector shifted uneasily at the table before wrapping his claws around the stem of a gilded cup. "Your eminence, I can assure you we have no problems. This is the lost princess from the kingdom of men, one who goes by Evie Mor, but I think we can bestow a more generous name upon her. I've picked out a few suggestions which denote her royal blood and her secret that she is a goddess blessed with magic from the gods."

His Eminence held up his hand to stop the triad of chatter coming from the Chief Collector. He extended a hand to the faun, all the while his dark eyes examining me. "Ohran, I'd like to hear what you have to say, and then I'd like you to remove the gag from this beauty. I want to hear her tongue and see her perform in the ring. We haven't had a human warrior for some time and the audience will go wild."

Ohran handed my leash to the Chief Collector; who held it between two fingers as though I were a poisonous viper that would sting him. I scowled as best I could at both the Chief Collector and His Eminence, which only caused more drool to drip down my chin. It itched as it slipped down my chest increasing my mild annoyance at not being able to wipe it away.

When Ohran placed his hands on the bare skin of my waist, I flinched. He turned me to the side and pointed. Without looking, I knew he'd revealed the mark on my skin. The jagged edges of darkness spread like a disease that would devour me if I did not find the cure. "She wears the mark of the angel of the death. You know well that his warriors are frequent guests in the arena, and should one of them see the mark, they will tell him we did not surrender her to him immediately. We do not wish to invoke the wrath of a powerful ally."

"I can assure you that all precautions were taken," the Chief Collector interrupted, a shuddering gait to his words. "We paid good money for her, and I am loath to lose it on what could be our most promising recruit yet. Yes, the angel of death may have marked her, but if we cover it up, no one will be the wiser. Your Eminence, you asked me, personally, to come up with a solution to change the arena to increase attendance and fill our coffers with coin. She is the solution. Pit her against the blue demon and the crowds will roar like never before."

"While that may be true, is it wise to invoke the wrath of the angel of death?" the faun asked skeptically. "We have had peace for twenty years, ever since the kingdom men fell. Would you risk it now?"

His Eminence flicked his hand, and the light glittering off his scales forced me to look away. "Why waste my time with this pointless bickering? Send a message to the angel of death and tell him we have secured his property. If he wishes to pay for her, he may, but I think he will be inclined to watch her in the arena. It will be far more interesting to see her fight without magic. Even more so if you give her back her sword."

My heart squeezed at the idea, and I tried not to give away both my dread and hope. I sensed that if I faced the angel of death again there would be no escape. But if I got my hands on the red sword, and it sang for me again, I might have a chance, however slight.

17

After the revelation of the mark and the decision to contact the angel of death, the faun took me back to my cell. This time, instead of being shackled to the bed, he attached my ankles to a short chain. It gave me enough room to walk between the bed, retrieve food when it was delivered, and use a bucket to relieve myself. Much like the days when I was Jezebel's prisoner, my time stretched into utter boredom and frustration. A cycle of endless thoughts plagued me. What I could have done to prevent my capture and how to escape before the angel of death arrived. I desperately did not want to see him again.

The way his dark eyes studied me, the fluid movements of his body, the way his tongue tasted, and the scent of his body. Dark. Intoxicating. My face flamed at the memory of the way I'd kissed him back. As though he'd pulled me under a seductive spell, and I couldn't help but respond. No, it wasn't what I wanted at all to be under his control, to become his dark queen, but try as I might, no opportunities for escape appeared.

I paced back and forth searching the dungeon walls for loose stones, soft mud, or any impurities that would allow me to dig. Closest to the bars was where I assumed the rock would be weakest. Someone had cut away rock to install the grate, but the short leash wouldn't allow me to reach them.

Instead, I waited, paced, and tried to be grateful I wasn't being bled, starved, or whipped. My thoughts bounced between imagining my upcoming reunion with the angel of death to wondering about Adomos and whether his fate was better than mine. When I met him again, I'd ask about the arena and the gladiators. Labraid was full of surprises, and my first journey did not even begin to cover the depth and magnitude of the many people who dwelled in Labraid.

A memory of Romulus came to me, his hand in mine, slowly growing cold as he spoke of the ice people. He'd wanted to liberate them from his mother. My sister wanted me to free her from the angel of death. And I no longer knew what I wanted. Short term, I wanted to be free, to find the red sword, and return to my quest to find my father with Adomos. Long term? The future hung before me like a veil of fog over the mountain.

My morose thoughts threatened to overwhelm me as I paced in silence. Bored. I wondered if this was how Adomos had felt in his cave, sitting in the dark, hiding from the world. Even though his imprisonment had been out of choice. What did he think of his situation, trapped underground, forced to train to become a gladiator? He had enough strength to protect himself from the worst, and I had trained with powerful centaurs. I should be able to fight and to keep my own among others. I wondered what monsters the collector kept in the dungeon for sport. I didn't hear any of them, which made me feel very alone.

Pausing, I sat down on the edge of the bed and ran my fingers down the chain, searching for a weakness in the links. I'd looked before, but there was none then and none that I could find now. I pulled at them, my frustration growing as the sound of footsteps echoed in the chamber. Low voices spoke in deep, guttural tones. I stilled and sat up straight, straining my ears to listen as they neared.

From the fluctuations of their tones, it sounded

as though they were arguing. They fell silent and a moment later, the key turned into the lock. The squeak of iron came as my prison cell opened. I leaped to my feet, my hands clasped in front of me, determined to look compliant even though my heartbeat swelled and flipped. If they were coming for me, it meant something had happened. Was he here? The angel of the death with his warriors?

It was the faun again, a deep scowl on his face, and with him was the Chief Collector, eyes darting over his shoulder constantly as though he were being watched. The tension between them was palpable, and I frowned right back at them. "What's going on?" I asked.

"Will you remain silent or do we have to gag you?" the faun asked.

"I'll be quiet," I blurted out not wanting to repeat the experience of the gag.

The faun grunted in response and began removing my chains from the wall and tying my hands in front of me. I allowed him to put a collar around my neck and attach the leash while the Chief Collector watched. Questions burned my throat, but I kept my eyes on the faun, letting my displeasure burn through.

"You haven't cleaned her up. He'll be displeased," the Chief Collector fretted.

"You should have considered that before you made an impulsive decision with the faerie," the faun snapped.

"I didn't know she was marked." The Chief Collector twisted his hands together.

The faun did not reply, and I gathered from their conversation that the angel of death was within the walls of the arena. A shiver of fear twisted through me as I recalled my initial meeting with him. I was at more of a disadvantage now, and I closed my eyes briefly. I was powerless with only my voice to bargain with. What promise did I have to make to get me out of this dire situation? All my life, I'd heard terrible things about Kedron Abbadon. He was a tyrant, a merciless enemy known for crimes across Labraid, and the one I needed to kill. But now it was more likely that he'd kill me first.

The faun led me out while the Chief Collector followed behind muttering under his breath and ignored by the faun and myself. Layers of halls, stairs, and dark passageways passed in a blur, and distantly came the sound of throbbing drums followed by a roar. "What is that?" I asked, forgetting to keep my mouth shut.

"Today the new contestants fight," the faun said.

I wondered if I would have been one of them had they not discovered the truth about me.

When the faun threw open a door, my stomach coiled. The sound of drums and the roar of the crowd rose to a deafening level as we entered yet another balcony. It was set up in the same way the previous one had been where I'd met His Eminence. He was in the room too, but my eyes were drawn directly to the Kedron Abbadon who stood with his back to me, his hands resting on the railing.

There it was again, that heavy scent of magic and the power of his presence. Dark and sensuous like a perfume spreading through the room. I wanted to spin around and flee, but my fingers itched for a blade.

He turned when the door opened as though he sensed my presence. When his soulless eyes met mine, a feral smile made his lips curl. I stared right back at him, knowing what I looked like. A slave. A far cry from the supposed dark queen he wanted. We watched each other, waiting to be the first to break the spell. When the faun yanked on the leash, I stumbled and lost eye contact.

The room was set up much the same with a banquet of food that made my mouth water. I'd lost weight in the prison because of their abominable food; a mush that left my jaw longing for something to bite into and a drink that would make me forget my circumstance.

Dancers weaved back and forth ignored by most. The rest of the people in the room leaned over the curved balcony, and I glimpsed sand and stone as the faun led me up to the top tier.

Kedron Abbadon spread his fingers with a flash of distaste crossing his face at the leash. "Chains are unnecessary here," he said, his voice a low growl. "Release her."

The faun's gaze shifted to His Eminence, who waved his hand in agreement. "Do as he says. Even if she runs, there is nowhere to go."

The faun reluctantly removed the chains around my arms and feet then, finally, the collar around my neck. I rubbed my wrists, briefly wondering if all magic was blocked down here and if Kedron Abaddon could use his.

"Come." Kedron Abbadon held out his hand to me, and I had no choice but to close the distance between us.

I positioned myself at his side holding myself stiffly, but his arm slid around my waist, regardless. "I came as soon as I heard about your predicament," he whispered in my ear as though he were a friend come to save me from the arena.

The familiarity with which he addressed me was both curious and irritating. I stiffened as his hand on my waist tightened possessively pulling me against his side. Out of the corner of my eyes, I noticed the Chief Collector, His Eminence, and the faun lean in almost hungry to see what would happen next. I did not enjoy being the source of their entertainment, and my jaw tightened.

"I wouldn't be in this predicament if not for you," I retorted.

"That is not entirely true, is it?" Kedron raised an eyebrow studying my face for a reaction.

I looked away unable to meet his gaze as a swirl of confusion rose in me. Instead, I stared out at the arena. "If not for you, I wouldn't have been forced to protect the defenders. It was your warriors who attacked me."

"I did not tell you to make a deal with the faerie. Did no one warn you of their treachery?"

"No," I said, keeping my answer short.

"You killed many of my elites. An impressive victory for you, but I believe you had some help." When I did not respond, he went on. "Where is the red sword?"

Finally, a question I could answer truthfully. "I don't know. Why don't you ask His Eminence."

"Because I prefer to hear your voice."

I kept my face forward determined to ignore him even though a muscle in my cheek jumped. Down below, I finally had a view of the arena and my lips parted. We stood on one of many covered balconies which enclosed the oval arena. Most of it was open to the air, and we were some stories high. Below us, rows of people filled the stair-like seats, and in the middle was a flat plain of sand.

Suddenly, I understood. During my time with the centaurs, I'd trained with the warriors. Sometimes, we'd form a circle and cheer on the trainees as they fought one-on-one. This was the same, but I sensed something malicious about this arena. The hollow bang of the drum. The roar of the audience as though they were thirsty for blood.

"This is your first fight, isn't it?" Kedron's question brought my attention back to him. "Would you rather be contending? They called me because you carry my mark, and it is my choice whether you fight to the death. But I could make it yours if you wish to join the heroes who have fought and won in this arena. Do you believe you are strong enough without magic?"

"Is that what you want for me? To die a bloody death in an arena?"

He brushed his mouth against my hair, the movement light and oddly intimate. "No, you know what I want from you."

I shuddered as the drums ceased and trumpets blared.

18

A deep voice bellowed across the stadium as the crowd went silent. Heads craned as they listened.

"To start off today's events, we have the hell dog Rip versus warrior Tartan."

The speaker continued, but the roar of the crowd drowned out his voice. My fingers tightened on the balustrade as—caught in the crowd's bloodlust—I strained for a better view. At the bottom of the arena, heavy gates swung open, and out trotted a three-headed beast. The announcer had called it a hell dog when, in the truth, the enormous furry brute was the size of a horse. Its three mouths formed into a snarl displaying sharp fangs as it barked. As the crowd continued to shout, it paced the oval growling and snarling.

The gates on the opposite side opened, and this time out strode a Lizdarian carrying a mallet. His muscles bulged and scars lined his scaly face, easy to see even at a distance. He thumped his chest as the crowd chanted his name. "Tartan. Tartan. Tartan."

He roared and slammed his mallet into the ground, sending a wave of sand toward Rip the hell dog. Bile rose in my throat. I knew what would happen next, and I didn't want to see it. But I forced myself to look. To endure what lay before my eyes, suddenly aware of my ignorance.

Labraid wasn't what I thought it was. Aye, the land was beautiful and fraught with magic and mystery, but underneath lay hidden layers of evil and corruptness. I wondered what the angel of death and his allies had done in the past twenty years that no one else knew about while the innocent and not so innocent suffered. I'd made a mistake in trusting the fey folk and I'd paid for it by becoming a prisoner of the arena. Had other fighters arrived similarly? The faun had explained it was a prison for magical warriors, yet I'd done nothing to incur imprisonment. How many others were innocent and forced to fight to the death?

The frenzy of the crowd swelled as the fight

began. Initially, I'd assumed the hell dog, Rip, would have the advantage, but his heavy body and three heads slowed him down. While Tartan was quick and made every blow count. Each wound made the hell dog angrier and violence and rage—not skill—guided his attacks. Bone snapped as Tartan took the advantage to bash in one of the dog's heads and break ribs. Streaks of bright blood and then teeth littered the sand.

My stomach churned in horror, but I could not look away as the gory violence played out before me. This was what the crowd had come to see and fear. Now, fury made me tremble. Wetness filmed my vision, and I blinked to clear the tears away hoping Kedron would not see my reaction. Was this what the people of Labraid had sunken to? Spectators of death cheering on another's demise? What was wrong with them?

Raising his mallet high, Tartan slammed it into the side of the hell dog. Rip went down with a thud, but Tartan did not stop. As the crowd roared, he brought his mallet down, again and again, to shatter bone and send spurts of blood flying until what had been the hell dog was only a bloody pulp. Pressing a fist to my mouth, I turned away weak and shaky. An itching came inside, and even though my magic wasn't supposed to work in the arena, I felt it deep inside, tightly bound, and begging to be freed.

Fingers under my chin drew my face up, and I struggled to keep tears out of my eyes as Kedron Abbadon, my enemy examined me. “This is not the kind of entertainment you enjoy, is it?”

I did not trust my voice, so I shook my head instead. I should not be indebted to Kedron Abaddon, yet the mark on his skin had saved me from becoming a contender and ending up like the hell dog, or worse.

Kedron Abbadon kept his voice low as he spoke words intended for my ears alone. “They say the sport is for men, for captains, warriors, and guards who understand the true meaning of fighting and what it means to live or die according to the whims of others. Watching the fights in this arena gives them a release because they understand that even though their days are numbered if they are sent here an honorable death can be earned.”

“There is nothing honorable about death here.”

“No? Would you rather be slain in battle? Beheaded based on some whim? Or fight to your death in the glory of the arena? At least then you have a choice of how you die, and you can use your wits and strength to live another day. Do you know what happens to the champions?”

I shook my head because I'd assumed they went back to their prison cells.

"Champions are treated like royalty and given food and drink, clothing, rooms, women, all that their heart's desire. But in order to keep that luxury, they must prove themselves to be winners over and over again. Such is the life of the warrior, Tartan. A crowd favorite. But will he keep his position as the champion? Or will someone else, someone new, take his place?"

I stared at Kedron as the trumpets sounded again, and the announcer bellowed out a name. A flash of blue and gold caught my eye and my heart constricted. Adomos strode into the ring, and a rush of fury and desire collided building into a storm within. It was as though all this had been orchestrated for me and me alone. As if Kedron Abbadon knew who Adomos was to me. I'd already watched Romulus die. I would not, could not, stand by and watch someone else I cared for perish because of my choices.

My jaw worked, and I glared at Kedron Abaddon. The darkness of his soulless eyes absorbed my anger. "What do you want from me?" I demanded.

"I want you to come with me willingly. Not as a slave, or a tool, or warrior, but because you desire to be with me."

Desire. Nothing within me desired him at all except for the pleasure of killing himself with the red sword. At least, that was the thought I struggled to cling to because another part of me speculated about things I should not think about. Like his tantalizing kiss and the invitation to become his dark queen.

I closed my eyes and felt as though Brianna stood before me begging me for freedom. I sensed that if I gave her what she wanted, she'd be the one to become queen, and I'd be the warrior standing by the side. Wasn't that what my mother had wished? For me to defeat the angel of death and become the protector? The defender of the people while my siblings reigned?

A bitter taste hung in the back of my throat, and I opened my eyes as the crowd roared eagerly for blood and battle. My voice rang out firmly even before I finished deciding. "I'll go with you, but only if you do one thing for me."

"Ask."

I pointed to the arena where Adomos stood, ready to fight Tartan.

"Set him free."

Kedron Abbadon's eyes lit up. "Set him free," he repeated. "Why? Do you care about the beast? A half-angel, half-demon, fallen from grace?"

"Is it so wrong that you would put down your own kind?" The words were out of my mouth before I thought, and the flash of irritation on his face told me I had struck true. The idea was impulsive. I weighed the meaning of it. Was Kedron Abbadon a Nephilim like Adomos? Half-angel and half-demon? It made sense. He had long life, some kind of magic I didn't understand and appeared ageless. My jaw tightened as I put the pieces together. He was tall, masterful, and smart in every way. He was no enemy I could overthrow quickly, but if I lived with him, agreed with him, and gained his trust, I could destroy him from the inside out. It was risky, and I wasn't sure if I had the strength within me to accomplish such a feat, but I felt the stirrings within. It was him or the arena.

Without waiting for a response, I tightened my fingers on the balustrade and leaped over it. A collective gasp filled the balcony and the guards stepped forward as I hung precariously on the other side. Keeping my gaze fixed on Kedron Abbadon, I repeated. "Set him free, or else I go to join him in the arena."

The side of his face curled up. He caught my bluff. Knew I wouldn't truly go down there without a weapon to fight against the champion. We both knew I'd die, and yet, it was a risk I had to take.

Kedron Abbadon held up a hand waving the guards away.

My lips moved to pray for the gods to see me, to hear me, for once. And then I leaped.

Falling hurt, but I caught myself on the railings and using handholds made my way down the columns while shouts and cries came. When I reached a level where people sat, I dashed down the steps fire burning within. I heard someone shout my name. "Evie! No!"

But it was too late. I leaped over the barrier and fell with a thump into the arena.

19

Gritty sand rubbed my skin raw as I rolled gasping for air. Pin pricks of pain spread across my body but I forced myself to stand. Adrenaline sent my minor discomforts to the back of my mind. Adomos spun in a whirl of gold and blue. His narrow golden eyes widened in recognition. With a nod, I tossed back my hair now tangled with sand. My poor excuse for clothing had twisted around me baring more of my skin. The crowd shouted enjoying the spectacle, and anger burned within me.

When Tartan roared and raised his mallet, I lifted my hands. The stink of blood and guts was thick in the air. The mutilated pulp of what had once been the hell dog was much worse close up. My control had snapped and nothing, not even the binding of my magic, could make me stop. It was still my magic, deep within me, and those who controlled the arena could not take away what was mine.

"Duck!" I screamed to Adomos, who twisted away from the blow.

Tartan thumped it into the ground and a wave of sand leaped around my ankles. Spreading my legs to keep my balance, I held my hands higher. But at first, nothing happened. The crowd calmed down then slowly chanted. "Tartan. Tartan. Tartan."

Magic quickened within and red flames burst out of my palms blazing crimson as they blasted into Tartan. Taken by surprise, he bellowed and staggered back. Lifting his mallet as a shield, he attempted to protect himself, but the river of fire consumed him burning relentlessly.

My ears rang and the beat of the drums. The roar of the trumpet and the shouting of the crowd sounded faint and far away. My rage turned toward them. Spectators of death. Spinning on my heel, I raised my hands again and aimed a river of fire toward them.

Chaos broke out as the arena caught fire. People ran, stumbling over each other in their haste to get away. The gates on both sides of the arena burst open with more contestants on the other side. Instead of running toward us, they turned on the guards, and a dark sense of victory rolled through me. Boldly, I lifted my gaze to the balcony where Kedron Abbadon stood watching. Waiting.

Lifting my fist, I hurled a ball of magic at him, but my strength wasn't enough and it fell, harmless, into the ground. In response, Kedron Abbadon's lips curled up in a wicked grin; sharp teeth glinting like fangs in the light. Despite the distance, I shivered but boldly lifted my chin. He'd seen what I had wrought and would not underestimate me again.

"Evie, we have to go," Adomos announced, his deep voice warm and comforting. Touching my hip, he turned me to face him and enveloped me in his arms. "Hold on," he instructed.

I'd never flown before, and I kept my arms around his neck while staring down at the destruction. Fire burned and occasional explosions shook the arena as we flew high above it into the coolness of the sky. As we soared into a cloud, death and fire and destruction faded from view. I hung on with a grim satisfaction rising within me.

It was a while before Adomos brought us back down to the ground. We landed near a shimmering body of clear water with redwood trees towered above hiding our presence. After battle and blood, the scent of cedar and pine along with cool mud beneath my feet calmed my racing heart. Adomos let go of me and stepped back, but relishing our close contact, I brushed my fingers down his arm. "Thank you."

He nodded somberly, holding my gaze. "Tell me, Evie, what happened? Why were you with the angel of death?"

My shoulders slumped, and I closed my eyes. My throat worked as I struggled to come up with the words. "It all started that day we went to the cave," I admitted.

"Tell me," he encouraged.

Adomos would not judge me, but it was too hard to look at him, so I paced as I explained everything. How Kedron Abbadon had set a trap for me, and how I'd fled to the Hall of Defenders with Takari and Romulus. I even shared the conversations I'd had with my sister, both before and after Romulus' death. I accepted the blame for my grief and anger, which led me to make a foolish deal with the faerie, and being traded to the arena. And finally, I showed him the mark and explained what Kedron Abbadon wanted from me. Relief filled me as I finished, as though I'd put down a heavy burden by confessing to Adomos.

When I finished my story, the silence stretched between us. The cool tang of pine and peppermint surrounded us along with the scent of water, reminding me that I needed to wash the filth of the arena from my skin. Somewhere far off, a bird called out and another answered. Peace surrounded us in the evergreen forest, and I lifted my gaze to the heavens searching for answers.

"I was captured too," the rumble of Adomos' deep voice was comforting and my shoulders relaxed. Moving to the shore, he squatted by the bank cupping a handful of cool water and splashing it on his face before continuing. "I believe the cave was a trap, and the warriors were already watching and waiting for us to make a mistake. The defenders confirmed what I'd guessed. That the elite warriors were prowling the wood for a while both aware the Hall of Defenders was nearby and guessing you might be headed that way. They killed for sport and left carnage to draw our attention. When the floor of the cave swallowed you, warriors came for me. We fought, but they weren't interested in killing me, only subduing me. They tied me up and took me to the arena, a three-day journey. I suspect the arena is buried under the same mountain range the defenders use."

I frowned. "Are we still in the mountains?"

"We are in the foothills. I did not take us far for two reasons."

"What are those reasons?" I asked joining him in

the lake. It was much colder than I'd expected, and within seconds, goosebumps pebbled on my arms. Holding my breath, I submerged myself scrubbing at my skin with the palm of my hand to get rid of the grit of sand and stain of blood.

When I rose out of the water, Adomos was on shore stacking wood. "We need to build a fire. You'll catch cold from the water, and you have no clothes."

Teeth chattering, I wrapped my arms around my body as I climbed onto the shore. My clothing from the arena was shredding, but regardless, it had been a pitiful excuse to keep me warm. I tossed a ball of fire onto the pile of wood. It sizzled, smoked, but finally, the wood burned.

Adomos added another handful of wood to the pile then wrapped his wings around me. He was solid, warm, and my heart beat faster at our skin-to-skin contact. A slight fluttering began in my belly as I leaned my head against his chest. Hidden in the shadow of his wings, I was warm and safe, as though nothing terrible could happen to me as long as I was with him.

"We're alone out here," Adomos said, chest rumbling as he spoke. "Without weapons, supplies, or clothes. Even though we are warriors, if attacked by the angel of death, we'll easily be overpowered.

You have to consider what to do next, return to the Hall of Defenders for supplies or. . ." he trailed off.

My eyelids were heavy as I leaned against him, my head swarming with everything that had happened today. Instead of thinking more, I wanted to rest without worrying about what the future held or my place in the world.

"Let's make camp here and rest," I suggested. "I'm not sure what I should do next, and you're right, we are in a difficult position. But this is the most comfortable I've been in weeks."

Adomos's arms tightened. "Rest, warrior princess."

My lips curved up in a smile and my heart skipped a beat as I sank into his warmth. It was the first time he'd called me a warrior princess, and I'd done something incredible today. I'd escaped Kedron Abbadon, and defied those who controlled the arena by using magic. I was stepping into my power, not as a warrior princess, but as a goddess.

20

The scent of roasted meat pulled me out from a deep slumber and I sat up, squinting in confusion. A softness covered me much like a blanket. It was night, dark, but a pool of white light shone over the lake and tiny fireflies hovered over the waters casting lights like golden stars. A smile crept to my lips as I stared at it; awed by the beauty of nature. The fire blazed much higher and hotter with a spit of meat roasting over it. On the outskirts of the light lurked Adomos's dark shape. He appeared like a giant as he returned from the trees carrying more wood and reminding me of my first glimpse of him. The blue giant was hidden in the shadows. He'd been sad then and quiet, unwilling to speak much at all. I still knew little about him and his past, but did it matter?

"You've been busy while I've slept."

"Aye, I found some travelers. Frightened them a bit," he chuckled, "but I only took what we needed. There are animals in the wood. If we forage and hunt, we will not starve."

"Thank you," I said eyeing the bundle of clothes. I picked out a tunic and quickly pulled it on before wrapping the blanket around my shoulders again. My stomach growled, no doubt in response to the meat.

Adomos sat down beside me facing the lake and fed more wood into the fire. I helped; snapping twigs and tossing them into the hues of orange flame. Satisfied the fire was in no danger of going out, Adomos sat back and I moved closer to him until our thighs touched. He responded by wrapping an arm around my shoulders hugging me tight and comfortable ease settled between us.

We watched the fireflies dance, and the wind created a ripple of tiny waves. A memory of a night in the Beluar Woods flashed in my mind. The voices of the centaurs singing, the humming of the creatures of the night, and the impenetrable circle of peace. I recalled Epona's words about returning to my birthplace if my adventure in the kingdom of men was not what I thought it would be. Sudden homesickness gripped me.

"I wish it could always be like this," I whispered.

Adomos grunted in response.

"The woods are peaceful, and it reminds me of Beluar. I felt safest in the forest because nature was my friend. The nights were beautiful, not quite like this though for I rarely saw the sky. I prefer seeing the stars, the moon, Mother Selas, the water, and the lights. It makes me feel like I belong out here in this great, beautiful world. A night like this gives me hope that Labraid is not full of dark and evil, and perhaps it is worth saving. After everything that has happened to me, it's hard to know what I believe anymore. The centaurs believed the woods are sacred, and the way of the gods is correct. But I'm a child of the gods, and I can't help but feel that they've forsaken me. Except tonight feels like a gift."

"Someone once told me that every day is a gift, and the gods give us a choice. The things that happened to you are out of your control, but Evie, you are a warrior. You overcome all obstacles. Perhaps it's not about what the gods want, but what you will do with the gift of magic given to you. You have the freedom to choose who you become and how your actions influence those around you. Today in the arena, it was your choice to join me, and it was your magic that saved us. You are stronger than you think even without the red sword."

I shuddered at the memory of the sword's hungry voice. "I don't know what happened to it. Part of me is relieved it is gone, but the other part of me knows I need it to defeat the angel of death. Adomos, I left the Hall of Defenders to find you. We have to go to Dun'gilly to meet my father because I need a strategy to wage war and free the kingdom of men. I believe the people should be free to govern themselves; not with a king or queen who will grow comfortable and give into corruption."

"Despite what you do, there will always be a need for defenders. Even if you fight the angel of death and defeat him, there will always be enemies. Like the lesser demons who haunt the hills of Elsdore, the contestants in the arena, and jealous goddesses like Jezebel causing chaos. Labraid needs defenders."

I sighed and tapped my fingers on my knee. "What would you do if you were me?"

"You are determined to kill him? Kedron Abbadon?"

His name sounded odd on Adomos's tongue and my heart kicked. I nodded, suddenly not trusting my voice.

"I imagine you're hoping for a war strategy, which is part of the reason you want to visit your father but not the entire reason. The problem is much smaller than you imagine. Yes, the angel of death has his armies and warriors. He has bargained and traded and made deals with queens and kings and wiped out many who oppose him. But while people fear his warriors, it is he himself who inspires fear. His very name makes others frightened of him because of who he is. The angel of death. If he is gone, his kingdom will fall and his armies will search for a new leader before descending into chaos."

I tilted my head back so that I could look up at him. He clenched his jaw as he stared across the lake as though the conversation made him uncomfortable. The moonlight highlighted the gold in his eyes. "How do you know all this?" I whispered. "It is obvious? Should I know this too?"

Adomos paused then shook himself. "Remember when we met? You asked about my past to hear my story, to feel some empathy, and create a bond between us."

"Aye," I nodded remembering a thread of unease growing at the ominous note in his tone.

"I used to serve the angel of death until I was allowed to leave. If you want to defeat him, your strategy will have to be the element of surprise as you did in the arena. He underestimated you and let you go. It won't happen again."

The truth of Adomos' words sank in, and I bolted up shaking his arm from my shoulders as I glared at him. Adomos, my Adomos, used to serve my enemy. The one who'd torn the kingdom from my mother and forced me to grow up with the centaurs believing I was unloved and unwanted by my parents. He had been part of it. Disbelief crowded my mind.

Romulus had warned me. I didn't know Adomos, and he was Nephilim, half-angel, half-demon. He had given into his dark tendencies and served. My entire body shook with shock and anger as I spun away from him and marched toward the lake. Had Adomos stormed the capital city? Had he chased down the king and queen? How many innocents had he slain?

The lake blurred as tears filled my eyes. Impatiently, I swiped at my cheeks with the back of my hands. Every time I thought I had life figured out, something else happened and the mental and physical shock of it sent me reeling. I wanted to kneel at the shore and rail at the gods, but this had been my choice. Adomos had warned me I would make enemies by his side, but I still chose him.

Bending over, I took a slow breath. Adomos had done nothing to harm me even though he'd had plenty of opportunities. I'd wanted to know his story, but I'd never have imagined this.

He was right, though. I had some control over my life, and I couldn't forget that I choose him and he swore allegiance to me. Instead of using my feelings, I had to use my head. His knowledge was an opportunity to end this reign of terror once and for all.

He waited patiently while I debated, and at last, I turned around. "Tell me, Adomos, tell me how to defeat him."

21

Adomos leaned closer to the fire with flames highlighting the runes on his dark blue skin. Despite what I'd just learned about him, a thread of desire pulsed under the surface. He was still the same Adomos I'd met before, but the knowledge of his past showed him in a different light.

Would that always be the case? The more I learned about someone's history, the more I'd judge them based on my view of the world? I didn't want to constantly worry that my friends might turn into enemies.

Using a stick, Adomos poked at the meat. Juice dripped down, spending sparks sizzling. When at last he spoke, his voice carried a strange note. "If you wish to defeat the angel of death, discover his weakness and find out what he wants. At one time, I believed it was the red sword, but he never acted upon the information he received about it. I left his kingdom years ago and do not know what plans have been discussed in secret."

"I know what he wants." The knowledge slammed into me like a punch to the stomach. "When I met him in the cave, he said he wanted me to become his queen. And again in the arena. He wants me. But why? That information does not help us."

Adomos rubbed his chin. "It does. We know he needs to fill a gap, and the answer is you, but that is not so surprising. Perhaps you were always what he wanted. He infiltrated the capital city before the king and queen fled, and when they did, he lost the trail. Supposedly, squads of warriors roam the land. Maybe they are searching for you."

I cocked my head, curious about the significance. "He let me go when I met him, though."

"Free will is important. He didn't want you to be forced to join him. He wanted you to make a choice of your own free will. If you've ever forced someone to do something against their will, you know how it feels. There's a hollowness associated with it, at least for those who haven't lost all their empathy. It is better to have a choice, especially in determining who will walk beside us."

He spoke matter-of-factly, but I didn't miss the hint of bitterness in his words. Crossing the ground in bare feet, I kneeled beside him and placed my hand on his shoulder. "Adomos, what you told me frightened me, but I understand that your past does not define you. You've had a change of heart since you left the service of the angel of death, and that is the reason I wanted you by my side. In my darkest hour, you saved me, and I will not forget that. You were the first to see me as more than a lost princess with the blood of the gods, and you gave me a chance to prove myself against Jezebel. I'm still young and have much to learn about the ways of the world, but I don't hold your past against you."

Adomos covered my hand with his larger one, his touch sending a blaze of warmth tingling to my toes. "Those words from your lips are more dear to me than all the treasure in the world. Many would hold my past against me, but to forgive as quickly and as easily as you did. Well, that is godlike."

I wrapped my fingers around his and squeezed. "It's difficult," I whispered. "But someone wise once told me I cannot go through life with hate in my heart."

His sad smile crossed his face for he was the one

who'd told me that. "It is a wise statement indeed. In the end, you only hurt yourself."

Nodding, I held his gaze. When he cupped my cheek with his free hand and bent his head closer to mine, I did not move away. Instead, I parted my lips and closed my eyes, waiting for that feather-light touch. When his mouth touched mine, the memory of Kedron Abbadon and what had taken place in the arena faded. That was only a hollow shell, a shadow of what could be. The bond Adomos and I shared was much more than a caress, a kiss. We both had darkness in our past, him more than me, yet we understood each other. I needed him because there was no one else. Leaning forward, I deepened the kiss. Even though I was inexperienced, my mouth knew what to do. Letting go of his hand, I rested my palms on his chest, feeling his heartbeat increase like drums, thudding faster.

We pulled back at the same time, panting, gasping. A low chuckled escaped from Adomos, a mirthful sound I'd never heard from him before. "You are quite passionate."

I grinned at him, feeling light and weightless. Hope filled me, such as I hadn't felt since my time in Anon Loam. "As I told you before, you're the only one I want on my side." Tilting my face to the sky, I inhaled the tranquil air. "Adomos, I think I know what I have to do, but I don't want to discuss it further tonight. Can we just relax and eat and talk about something else? Tell me a tale, a story that ends in happiness."

"I'm sure you know many more tales than I do, especially from your time with the centaurs. Why don't you tell me one of those?"

I smiled. "My favorite is the legend of Druantia, the goddess of the forest, and how she coaxed the wood nymphs to awaken and brought life to the forests."

"Tell me," Adomos coaxed, pulling the meat off the fire.

And so I did.

WE RESTED BY THE LAKE, not just for one night but for three days. The presence of the wood soothed me as though all time had stopped and I was allowed to rest and watch spring blossom. Green buds appeared on the trees, the promise of new life, and a tree by the waters bloomed with orange flowers. I made traps out of sticks, hunted in the wood, and forged for the light bounty the forest provided to eat. The lake was a better source of food providing fish we wrapped in leaves and cooked in the hot coals.

Adomos scouted while I hunted, reporting back that there was no movement in the woods, but we both knew our sabbatical was temporary. Soon it would be time to go. The truth about what I had to do whispered in my mind. The only way to win was to do as Adomos suggested and give the angel of death what he wanted before pivoting and using the element of surprise to take him down.

My side ached whenever I thought of him, but I refused to lift my tunic and watch the black mark spread. His mark. If only I could stay in hiding with Adomos, but I knew it was not to be. Too many people suffered while I hid. Eventually, the storm would break and the angel of death would demand I make a choice.

On the fourth morning, I woke to red dawn with my back warmed by Adomos' bulk. Today was the day. It was time.

"Adomos," I said to see if he was awake.

"Aye," he grunted.

"How far away is the capital city of the kingdom of men?"

He was quiet for a moment and then asked, "What are you going to do?"

"What I should have done a long time ago."

Sitting up, I faced him. "It's time for the rule of the angel of death to end, and I need your help."

Adomos listened while I explained my simple plan. When I was done, he nodded. "I will do my part, but Evie, you know not what you walk into. You will be alone."

"Aye, but my entire life, I've been alone. Others have encouraged and supported me, and even with the centaurs, I sensed there was more. It was only meant to be a temporary haven and to prepare me for the next step in my journey of life. I want to travel on to Dun'gilly and find my father, but the journey will only delay me. The darkness that spreads through Labraid has had a grip for well over two decades, and it's time for it to end. I can't stand by and let the world rot because I want to find myself first. Ever since leaving the Beluar Woods, I've tried to figure out who I am, why I'm here, where I belong. But the truth is, I was born to be different. Given the blood of the gods, so I could rise stronger and use my magic to save Labraid. If I don't go now, when?"

Adomos held me tight. "I've always admired your courage, but this is the right choice."

"Then you believe I will succeed?"

"I believe there is a chance. It will be tough, but

hold on to what you believe, and I will be out there, waiting for your signal."

Hues of pale pink light lit up the dark corners of the forest and shimmered on the lake as the sun rose. I tried to memorize it all and hold on to the sense of purity and freedom. I was doing this for Labraid, for my family, and for all the people who were afraid to walk outside and see the world as I could see it. Despite their beginnings, everyone deserved the chance to be free.

22

To speed our journey, Adomos flew high above the clouds where we wouldn't be seen by those below. We alternated between flying and resting, and at night found a hiding place. Adomos was skillful at finding a hollow in a tree, an empty cave, or, once, even the nest of an eagle. I'd never seen the world from such a height, and it was breathtaking and beautiful. Groves of trees appeared like emeralds in a distance, and the winding waters twisted like a clear path, leading to a hidden treasure. Was this why the gods always lived in high elevations? That they might look down at the world and approve of its natural beauty?

The landscape quickly changed with shades of spring deepening in a melody of colors, and suddenly in the distance, the capital city rose. Tears blurred my vision, forcing me to catch my breath as I stared at my birthright, but as I looked at it no sense of jealousy came over me. My mother had called it a prison, and I wondered if I'd draw the same conclusion when I entered.

Towers winked against the light and in a flash; it reminded me of a dream of long ago. I stood on the shore watching the ships come in, and above me flew blue devils. They came to destroy, and in my fear, I wanted to run and hide. But now I knew who I was and understood my power. Even when it should have been repressed, it came roaring out of me.

I clenched my fists. And just for a moment, I wanted to change my trajectory, but I would not turn back. I would not let the people of Labraid suffer as I did. Helpless, homeless, without a family.

Adomos's hand at my waist brought me out of my thoughts. "We can wait longer. We don't have to go today."

"No." I shook my head. "I want to go before I lose my courage."

With a nod, he wrapped his arms around me letting me face the world. I held onto his arms—not because I was afraid of flying, Adomos would hold me secure—but more to balance myself for what was to come. We lifted above the treetops and the tiered city rose before us. Gray walls towered on three sides. Level after level rising high into the sky as though it tried to reach the clouds yet failed. I counted the sections as we neared, and the shape of the city became clearer. Five levels to the capital city, which sloped upward built into a cliff.

From what I'd been told about the city, it backed up to the edge of the Labraid and the castle had a sheer drop off to the waters far below. Waters that hadn't been explored. Rumor had it if one sailed too far, they'd reach the end of the world and slip off the edge down into the underworld. It was easy to believe those tales were true as I stared at the city. My heart skipped a beat, and my eyes widened. This was the first man-made city I'd ever seen, the kingdom of men, and it was far larger than anything I'd ever imagined. Even from the air it spiraled, buildings rising and falling, many hidden by bridges, staircases, and towers.

It was only when a blue tower winked that I stilled, reminded of my dream—or had it been a vision? A blue castle towered at the summit of the city. Around it swarmed winged creatures too far away to make out. My breath hissed out as I made out the walls, wide enough for horses and chariots and warriors to march upon. It swelled up and down, surrounding the city as a firm and impenetrable barrier. How had Kedron Abbadon taken this city and how had any escaped? From the sky, it appeared as though no one could touch it. My stomach dropped; I could see no way in. And when I squinted, I could just make out the guards on the wall, pointing in our direction.

"Adomos, they've seen us," I called, the wind tearing at my words.

"I see," he replied.

His deep voice was calm, collected, as he barreled toward them. Blood roared in my ears and my heart skipped. I was making a mistake. We had to turn back. I'd be caught. Would Kedron Abbadon's armies respect the mark of the angel of the death and take me directly to him? Was he even home, back from his reign of terror? It was possible that was he still out there, searching for me. Never dreaming that I'd willingly walk into his lair.

"Remember what we discussed," Adomos said sensing my panic. "They will come for us, but that is what we want. To draw them away from their posts and cause a stir in the city, all eyes on us."

I took a deep breath. In the woods, it was easy to plan and imagine myself boldly striding into the kingdom, convincing Kedron Abbadon I'd come of my own accord, and then find the red sword. It meant I had to be uncomfortable for a while and cautiously hide my emotions because it wasn't war but a path of deception. I'd chosen this strategy because there was no time to raise an army and brutally take the kingdom by force. I was certain that path would lead to more deaths than I'd wanted.

My time in the castle would be temporary. All I had to do was keep my plan in the forefront of my mind and wait for an opportunity. Squeezing Adomos's arms, I let my mind drift back to our camp at the lake and our four days of relative normality. I locked the memory in my mind like a treasure. I'd return to it again and again when I needed some encouragement and to remember I wasn't alone.

"Are you sure?" I called out even though we'd already discussed the plan at length. "Are you sure they will believe you're turning me in, and that they'll let you go free?"

"They don't know what happened at the arena. They have no reason not to believe me."

"I need this to work," I whispered. "I need you."

"It will."

Adomos's words were sure and steady. I wondered if he knew with certainty that I could defeat the angel of death, or if he only hoped while hiding his true feelings from me. Again, he was difficult to read, but I trusted him. I had to have faith if I were to complete this ordeal.

"Shield!" Adomos roared.

My eyes flew open and magic surged within. We were much closer to the walls, and I could make out the shapes and sizes of the creatures below me. They were not humans, but guards who appeared demonic, half breeds, mutants, some big as giants, and some small with wings on their backs. This was what had become of the city. It was overrun with foulness, but as I lifted my hands and engulfed us in a shield of magic other people appeared below.

Humans, I was sure of it, even though they kept their faces pointed toward the ground. Questions arose in my mind as we passed. I'd never sat down to consider how the kingdom of men had fallen. Just that it had, forcing the king and queen to flee. But what if others hadn't been so lucky, and they'd become prisoners of this city? What had the angel of death done with them?

A high-pitched scream echoed around me as a ball of fire arced toward us. Despite the shield, Adomos ducked, but out of the corner of my eye, another one bloomed. This one crashed into the shield, knocking us off course. I felt the heat of the fire through my shield and even though Adomos told me not to retaliate, I wanted to. Instead, I focused on pouring energy into the shield and holding it steady.

Adomos took us higher as arrows pointed up at us, and then a shout came, splitting the air. My ears rang with the strength of it, and I recoiled almost forgetting about my magic. My limbs trembled as a boom shook the skies and then a bolt of lightning shot through it. The flash of fire so hot that the heat of it stung the hairs on my head.

Adomos dropped out of the sky as if he'd been hit, and a wall of stone rose to greet us. Adomos pulled up before we struck, but before he regained his balance and took us up into the skies again, guards surrounded us. Shakily, I faced them and, as Adomos backed against the wall, I swallowed hard. The sharp edges of spears and swords pointed at us, and even if I were to summon all of my magic we wouldn't escape alive. We were trapped.

23

"Halt in the name of the king!" A guard bellowed riding through the guards on a black horse.

Adomos glided out from behind me and spread his arms to hide me from the curious eyes of the guards. "Don't you recognize an ally when you see one?" He said, an angry lilt to his tone. "The angel of death will be furious to hear you blasted me out of the sky and almost destroyed the very one he seeks."

The guard on the horse frowned, surprised at the response. Quickly regaining his composure, he placed a hand on his sword hilt in warning. "It is forbidden to fly over the city. We are instructed to take down any we don't recognize."

Adomos lifted his chin. “Do you recognize me?”

“No, although you look like one of us. Who are you?”

“Escort us to the castle. I bring the angel of death a gift.”

The guard raised an eyebrow and peered around Adomos to get a better look at me. “Her?”

“She carries his mark.”

“We’ll see what he has to say,” The guard warned.

“Wait.” I stepped forward, ignoring Adomos. “Since I’m here, I’ll present myself. I don’t need an escort.”

A small rumbling began among the guards as they looked at each other.

“Who is she?”

“Why does the angel of death want her?”

“Wouldn’t it be best to kill them?”

I hesitated, wondering if I should lift my tunic and show them. But I also didn’t want to bare myself in front of so many strangers. But was it worse than what I was walking into?

“Come,” The guard on the horse said at last.

Kicking his mount, he led the way up the road to the castle. The brisk walk gave me a better view of the capital, and I lifted my head taking in the city that should have been my home. Away from the walls, the city spiraled out with a series of roads leading into tunnels and alleyways. Bridges were overhead where horses and riders and wagons and people walked or rode. Sometimes the castle was hidden from view, but most of the time edges of it appeared, rising high above all. A symbol of power that was even more terrifying from the ground.

The path curved and rose, taking us higher until we reached a bridge arching over a body of water. My lips parted as heavy iron gates opened. Trellises covered with statues of winged creatures with tails and horns carried swords and bows. This did not look like the kingdom of men but a haven for darkness. I walked into its midst determined to retain my sanity and withstand what was to come. My heart pounded as we entered the hall lined with guards. One stepped forward with hands raised to halt us.

I barely heard the quick conversation between two armored men, but when I turned to look back at Adomos, he was already being escorted out the gates. He glanced back at me and gave a swift nod so tiny, I wondered if I'd imagined it. But it was all the encouragement I needed. I lifted my chin and squared my shoulders searching for my inner peace. Here everything was out of my control, but the one thing I could control was my reactions. I was here to do one thing. What I had been born and bred to do my entire life: kill the angel of death.

If my speculations were correct, after what had happened in the arena, Kedron Abbadon would have transported the red sword to a treasury in the capital. A way to entice me back to him. And I wondered about what Adomos had told me. Why did the angel of death desire me and what did he need me for? The only reasoning I could come up with was the same reason Jezebel had hunted me down. For my blood. But the angel of death was already free to come and go as he pleased. He had the kingdom of men and ruled with a firm hand. His armies were feared across Labraid and nothing stood in his way, so what could he possibly want with me?

I stood in the hall a long time, the eyes of the guards boring into me as I clenched my fists and tried to keep my inner peace. When footsteps sounded on the gold floor, I almost breathed a sigh of relief. But it wasn't him. A tall woman with a cloud of black hair strode toward me. A red gown was wrapped tightly around her willowy body. Her pale face had sharp cheekbones and her dark eyes were accented further by her lips, which had been painted a dark color. A coldness emitted from her as she examined me. Flipping open a fan, she waved it at me. "Who are you?"

"I've come to see the angel of death," I faltered taken aback by her blunt greeting.

She waved the fan impatiently. "Many come to seek his favor, but why you, and why now?"

I licked my lips. "He has something I want."

A smirk crossed the women's face. "You're her, aren't you? The lost princess come to regain her kingdom?"

I went cold at the way she jested as though I were nothing but a joke. "I don't have an army."

"No, you've come to throw yourself at his feet? To be charmed by him, is that it? Why else would you walk into the heart of the kingdom barefoot, weaponless?"

Each word from her lips felt like a jab, and my head pounded with the beginnings of a headache. "I met him before in the wild. He asked me to come. He offered me something. . ." I trailed off because I hadn't expected to explain myself to this woman.

"Come, you cannot stand before the king dressed as you are, in rags. My servants shall purge you and then you can explain to him why you are here." Her lips curled up into what could not be called a smile, but glee, as though I were walking into a nasty surprise.

I hadn't expected this either, but I calmed my rising anxiety. I'd assumed Kedron Abbadon would be pleased to hear of my coming and rush to my side ready to protect me from the creatures within his castle. But that was not the case.

The woman turned on her heel, and I followed her deeper into the maze of the castle.

The lower levels were simple. Home to the guards or servants who roamed the halls, who ignored our passage. But as we ascended higher and deeper into the castle, the decor changed. Rich tapestries hung from the walls with depictions of battle and blood and great wars. I spared a passing glance at them but hastened to keep up with my guide. Stone floors gave to plush carpets, and we passed opened halls where people stared back at us. Women with fine gowns tittered behind fans while gallant men laughed while escorting them from room to room.

For a moment, I recalled my time with the elves and their abode, which intertwined with nature. This was much different, yet still, it was full of life. I considered of the rumors of corruption in the capital city, but within the castle were more humans than I'd dared to imagine. They lived alongside the angel of death and his armies. Could they not see what they were part of? But perhaps they did not wish to see because they were the ones who had betrayed the kingdom and given it over to new hands. The consideration that possibility left a sour taste in my mouth. I had no friends here. I needed to rely on my wits while Adomos did his work from the outside.

The decor changed again, and it became quieter as we entered a dark hall full of rooms. Here, torch-light lit the way. There were no windows open to the daylight. The root of fear snaked its way through me. At last, the woman pulled a set of keys from her belt and unlocked the doors. I tried not to think about why they were locked as she threw them open.

"These will be your rooms, as long as you're staying here," she announced.

I nodded, staring at the finery. This was more than what I'd had in Anon Loam. A bed made with frills and lace large enough for four or five to sleep on, plush pillows atop couches, and a table and chairs in front of the fireplace that took up almost an entire wall. Curtains on one side of the room revealed a balcony, but the glass doors that led outside were closed. A small door on one wall opened to an adjoining chamber. The empty wall space was covered with paintings, and when I lifted my head, my mouth dropped at the scenery which covered the ceiling. Who had taken the time to paint such an intricate scene in an unused room?

The woman rang a bell summoning servants to

her aid. Not one, but three, women appeared. They were smaller than her with their hair braided tightly around their heads. The woman waved a hand. "Prepare her for the king."

They descended upon me before I could speak or protest. I clenched my fingers into fists as a reminder not to use magic even though it bubbled inside me. They were only workers, not my enemies. They moved quickly in rotation. One went to the adjoining room, a washroom, and turned on the water, which filled a tub. Two approached me whisking me out of my clothes.

Even though my face flamed with heat, they showed no embarrassment as they guided me into the tub. Rose petals floated on the water, which smelled like rose, lavender, and something else I could not place. I leaned back under the suds and let them scrub the filth from my skin. Was this how royalty was treated? Waited on hand and foot so that they had nothing to do with themselves?

After the long bath, they dried me off and braided my hair in a series of complicated twists, leaving some loose hanging down my back while they braided the rest like a crown around my head. Finally, they dressed me in a pale green gown as soft as down feathers. It clung to my hips and dipped low in the front clearly displaying the swells of my breasts. I swallowed hard as they fitted me with shoes with a heel. The entire outfit felt odd, forced, but when they put me in front of a mirror, I drew a deep breath.

Somehow, they'd transformed me from a rough warrior into a princess. My red hair was tamed, showing off my long neck. The green of the dress highlighted my eyes, and the cloth accented my curves. I'd never considered myself beautiful or worthy of desire, but looking in the mirror, I realized that I appeared like a queen. A young one, nevertheless, but with a crown, I could see myself ruling.

"Come," The sharp voice of the woman cut through my thoughts. "The king awaits you."

24

Marble columns and gold statues lined the hall of the king along with portraits and paintings of lewd scenes that made my face go hot. The woman who led the way set a quick pace, and I stumbled in my heeled shoes. Wobbling as I attempted to keep up with her. A few times I stumbled on the sweeping hem of my pale green dress catching myself before I ripped it.

We paused in front of gilded doors and guards—who stood on either side—pushed them open as we appeared. Silver armor covered their entire bodies hiding their faces, but I noticed the mark of the angel of death, a jagged bolt of lightning, on their helms. I recalled the flash of light I'd seen in the sky as Adomos and I flew over the capital, but that memory faded as I entered the room.

I'd assumed it would be the throne room, instead, it was a private chamber with a balcony overlooking the cliffs and a view of the turquoise sky warmed by honey tinted rays of sunlight, that danced in and out of fluffy clouds. Natural light filled the room with brightness and glistened off the marble statues and cherry wood of tables and chairs. Stacks of books and scrolls lined one wall, while on the other side—with a clear view of the balcony—was a couch with thick gray furs draped over one side.

My eyes widened as I inhaled a light scent with hints of wood, fruit, and ink. I hated to admit it, but the chamber, filled with furniture, had a comforting allure to it. I longed to sit down, unroll a scroll, and lose myself for hours. The lack of fire left a slight chill in the room, but I supposed that was what the furs were for. My focus was fixed on the room. When the woman spoke I startled; I hadn't realized we weren't alone.

"My king, here is the princess, as requested."

"My thanks, Lady Enyd. That will be all. We will join you in the dining hall this evening."

Enyd, what a lovely name. She slipped from the room, and I bit my tongue to keep from begging her to stay. Kedron Abbadon was the entire reason I'd come to the capital, and yet the idea of being alone with him unnerved me. The dress felt tight and my face warmed as my exposed chest rose and fell. I was dressed like royalty, and this was my birthright. As firstborn, I should rule, so why did I feel so awkward?

A shadow rose from the balcony. No wonder I hadn't seen Kedron at first. He'd been sitting outside, just out a view. Now he entered the room, carrying a thick scroll in one hand and a silver goblet in the other. I sucked in a deep breath and pinched myself to regain my composure. He was just as I recalled him, clothed in all black. Those deep eyes seeking mine. His expression was stoic. Instead of a crown, a golden band encircled his head but heavy rings glinted on his fingers twinkling the stones caught the light. He moved like a king, calm and sure of himself. Placing the goblet on a nearby table, he approached me.

My stomach fluttered as his presence wrapped around me like a blanket, and again came that strange magic that emanated from him. I sucked in a deep breath to calm my nerves as he glided up to me. His gaze lingered on the bare skin of my chest as he extended a hand.

I hesitated, but only a moment, before allowing

him to take my hand. He lifted it to his lips and pressed a warm kiss against my palm. I shivered as though he'd imprinted me with yet another mark, and suddenly, it was difficult to breathe. We were alone, but not like it had been in the cave when I was determined to fight. This time I'd walked into his domain with one purpose, yet the idea of completing my task was far, far away.

"Have you come to kill me?" he purred.

I could not deny the effect his voice had on me. The tone sent a quickening through my lower belly. The hard truth stung because deep inside I knew I was attracted to my greatest enemy. And while I had to kill him, I also wanted to kiss him. Perhaps others had fallen under his spell, which is how he'd wormed his way into the hearts and minds of so many. I tried to think of how he was to blame for so many deaths. The squads that roamed the countryside attacked on whim. The elites that swarmed the hillside mutilating bodies. The reports of lesser demons with their numbers growing as the angel of death encouraged darkness to spread across the land.

"I have," I answered sincerely. "I came because you are right. There is no other way." Those words hurt to say even though they were true, too. "I came to be your dark queen and change the course of history. Your rule cannot continue like this. People are suffering, dying, and I would see that change. Recall your armies, return them to the capital, and leave Labraid in peace. I shall give you what you desire."

His fingers tightened around mine as he studied me as though he could peel back the layers of my mind to understand my motives. Yet everything I'd said was true. Unlike the elven queen, he did not use mind control on me. Instead, his gaze penetrated to my soul and, under his scrutiny, it became even harder to breathe.

"You are too innocent to come up with a devious plan. Every word you speak is the truth," he finally declared.

I nodded. "It is. You are my foe, but you have decades of experience." Adomos had coached me on flattery, subtly weaving it in between with the words I spoke. "My lack of knowledge cannot compare to your wisdom, and so I came to bargain because I assume you will not stop."

"No," his voice dipped. "I will never relent."

Letting go of me, he walked further into the room and gestured to the sitting area. "Come, sit, drink. Let us discuss terms of peace."

I sank into a pile of furs, eager to give my feet some relief from the shoes that pinched my toes. To my dismay, Kedron Abbadon sat down beside me leaving little room between us. From a table in front of the couch, he poured sparkling liquid into a goblet and handed it to me. I took a tentative sip unsure what it was and half wondering if he intended to poison me. But it was light, fresh with a hint of honeysuckle. The first sip bloomed on my tongue, and I took another, deeper one for strength.

When I dared to face Kedron Abbadon again, he was watching me intently. "Princess Evie, tell me, what do you want?"

I faltered while watching the fall of his raven black hair. How unfair was it for someone so evil, so deadly, to be so alluring? I bit my lower lip. "I've already told you. Recall your armies. Let the people of Labraid go free, and I will give you what you want."

One lip curled up. "What do I want?"

"I don't know." I stared at the shimmering liquid. "But I guess it involves me."

"You guess right."

One finger came under my chin turning me to face him again. He was so close, too close. His face was mere inches from mine showing me into the depths of his orbs of darkness. My heart hammered in my chest and my lips parted as a small sound escaped my throat. I hadn't meant to whimper, but the way he teased me, touched me, left me out of my depth.

"Our introduction to each other was awkward, wasn't it?" he went on. "You tried to kill me. I tried to seduce you. Let's forget the past, let bygones be bygones, and start over. You are the princess of the kingdom of men, Evie Mor. And I am the king of the kingdom of men, Kedron Abbadon. You will call me Kedron. There is no need to stand on ceremony, at least not when we are in private, like this. I want you to be my queen, to marry me, and seal the bond between the old kingdom and my new kingdom. As a wedding gift, I will withdraw my elites back here to the capital city. But I warn you, armies are made for war, and what use is there for them in a time of peace? If I don't send them forth to conquer a new territory, they will become restless and stir up chaos in the city. What answer do you have for that?"

Unable to hold his gaze, I closed my eyes with my mind reeling from his words. Marriage. To the angel of death. He's said it so quickly, so smoothly, as though it were just as simple as writing my name.

"It is difficult, is it not? To come to an agreement without the support of a father?" he purred.

The warmth made my chest constrict and my eyes flashed. I glared at him, suddenly bold. "And whose fault is that? You're the one who stole the kingdom from the king and queen."

"True, but they refused to make a deal with me." His gaze hardened. "What do you suppose your life would have been like if I hadn't stepped in? Do you think the king would have allowed you to live? One look at you and he would have known you weren't his child. Even if you'd been allowed to live, what do you think would have happened to the queen? Her treachery would have required punishment. Perhaps her head cut off in front of the people of Labraid? It would have been a party. All come to see the queen beheaded. What do you know about the ways of the men? About ruling a kingdom?"

He was baiting me, but I would not rise to his attack. "You've already won. We aren't debating the past, but the future. Dismember your armies, give them their lives, and let them walk free."

"Do you think they will repent? Forsake their ways? No, they are killers and that will never change. Would you have killers go free into Labraid? Don't you recall the arena and what happened there? It is a prison for murderers, and you freed one of the most dangerous ones. An elder demon, and yet you did not seem concerned about aiding him. If I had to guess, you care for him."

Anxiety wormed its way through me, and I

bounced my knee up and down unable to stop. I did not want to talk about Adomos, but Kedron stared at me so intensely I was forced to speak. "It was a favor for a favor."

"Ah, but I understand he was the one who turned you into me."

"Aye." I did not know how to lie, so I took another sip of the liquid. Bubbles fizzled down my throat and danced in my belly only adding to my nervousness.

"I've underestimated you once, and I will not do so again. If indeed, the elder demon is a friend of yours, you and I are not so unalike. Regardless, I will have him barred from the capital. I let him go free once, and he no longer serves me and will never do so again."

My plan was unraveling faster than I expected, but I had to stay calm. An opportunity would present itself. I just had to be patient as Adomos had advised me. Changing the topic, I spoke quickly, before I lost my courage. "If I marry you, will you give me the red sword?"

Now he smiled. "The red sword is not mine to give. It is already yours."

"But you brought it here from the arena?"

"I did. I admit as a lure. Hoping to bring you to my side. It worked, did it not?"

"Why me? You are much older than I, and surely there are many women to choose from?"

"True, but Evie, you are one of a kind. Not only are you a child of the kingdom of men, but you are a goddess, which will make you the most powerful queen Labraid has seen. Don't you want it? Power, authority, wealth, protection? I can give you all of it, as my queen."

I swallowed hard because he was right. Becoming his queen would give me back part of what I'd lost, but only part of it. This was all wrong. I didn't want to rule like this. I didn't want to become enslaved to his seductiveness, and yet I could see no way out of the trap I'd fallen into. Letting the silence stretch, I stared at the goblet willing it to give me an answer and show me another way.

25

I knew little about marriage ceremonies, but from the rumors I'd heard, they were celebratory events that took a while to plan. Agreeing to marry him would be a sign of trust, a bond between Kedron and me. It also gave me time to find the red sword and discover what secrets he might be hiding. Although the castle was vast and spiraling, impossible to uncover in the short time I had. But I'd come for one reason, and I could not back down even if it meant signing my life away. If my luck held, everything would be over before we were married.

He waited patiently beside me, drinking from his goblet. When I glanced at him out of the corner of my eyes, he was staring at the sky, lost in thought.

The calmness of his expression surprised me, and I was awed by how kingly he appeared. I tried to remind myself that he was years older than me, but I kept circling back to the fact that he was immortal, as was I. The blood of the gods made us so, and perhaps we were more alike than I expected.

"I want it in writing. All the things we'll both agree to should we marry," the words rang out crisp and clear on my tongue. "I want it signed, sealed with our blood."

"So you agree of your own free will?"

"I do."

Sitting down the goblet, he pressed his thigh against mine and curled his fingers around my neck, tilting my head toward his. Instinctively, my hands circled his wrists, but he did not squeeze. He searched my eyes, studying my face for any sign of treachery. But he would find no lie in my gaze, only a hint of anxiety because I'd given him the truth.

"I look forward to knowing you," he said.

When he pressed his lips against mine for the second time since we'd met, I responded. I hadn't intended to, but he tasted dark and sweet. His hands on me, claiming me, desiring me left me with a sensation of security and belonging. A feeling I'd been searching for ever since I'd left the Beluar Woods, and one I assumed I'd gain when I found my mother. Until I learned the truth and a jealous goddess snatched me away from her. But this was the truth, and the kiss was more than just a kiss. It was a promise, a bond. A union between us.

He forced his tongue between my lips, and I welcomed his intrusion. When I closed my eyes, I was lost in his caress, his touch. And although I wanted it to be right, deep inside, I knew it was very wrong. He was like the others, using me for his personal needs, and yet it didn't feel like that at all. It felt true and real, as though perhaps we were lost with a void inside that could not be filled, except with each other.

He broke the kiss first and released my neck. I brought one hand to my lips, which burned as if I'd pressed my lips against hot coals. I leaned into him, breathing hard, trying to regain my sense of self.

"You feel it too, don't you?"

"What?" I gasped, unable to look at him.

"What is between us? It blazes inside you too. I knew when I met you that you wouldn't be like any I've met before. A proud princess, a fierce warrior, a treacherous enemy, and a passionate lover. I'm tempted to take you now, but it will be more delicious to wait."

His raw words were like an unveiling. "Have you been searching for me? Waiting for me?"

Cocking his head, he studied me. "I have. I've been waiting for you to grow up, to reappear."

"You've wanted me to be your queen all along? But why?"

"Why indeed? I shall show you, but first, we have a contract to sign and a celebration to attend. Tonight, we announce our betrothal."

My throat went dry because I couldn't delay the inevitable. The knowledge that he both desired and wanted to marry me was flattering. Our union would be a powerful one and none would stand against us. But I was more than aware of the fact that he was my enemy and I should hurl a ball of fire into his face. But my magic did not sizzle inside. I had no desire to hurt or harm him. Why? Where had my resolve gone?

Taking my hand, he stood, pulling me up beside him. Again, I was keenly aware of his height and the broadness of his shoulders. He led me over to a desk and sat down behind it, pulling out parchment and ink. Flourishing the quill, he wrote. His words were a swirl of fine letters much better than any handwriting I possessed. When he finished, he turned it toward me and waited.

I read the words, my lips moving as I clenched my fingers together, grateful that I'd learned how to read faster and write better in Anon Loam. The contract read correctly, my demands and his written together. I nodded at him. "This will fulfill what I want, but I noticed you said nothing about the red sword."

"And I will say nothing about it. As I mentioned earlier, it already belongs to you and cannot be given as part of a blood contract."

I nodded in understanding. I'd find that sword wherever he'd hidden it. "How long will the wedding preparations take?"

His eyes lit up. "You are in a hurry?"

"No," I said hastily, correcting my mistake. "I'd like to take time. . .for us to take our time before we wed."

"Then we shall." He picked up a letter opener and held it up, then neatly sliced his palm. Dark red blood pooled on the parchment. Dipping a finger into it, he sighed his name then held out the letter opener to me.

I sliced through my palm quickly, ignoring the burn as I made a fist and my blood joined his. I signed my name, watching as our signatures flared up briefly, as though the joining of two set fire to the contract. Instead of burning, it smoked and the scent of scorched parchment filled the air.

I glanced at Kedron, whose expression was blank, and my heart throbbed. I blinked hard to keep tears from forming as waves of panic threatened to take over. What had I done? This was forbidden evil, and yet I'd joined myself with him. Even though my intentions were pure, I felt as though a piece of myself had been signed away, stolen by the angel of death. I stepped back wanting to run away, to escape his presence, but he was still there.

Pointing toward the balcony, he said, "There is a basin. You may wash the blood away and bandage your hand."

Spinning away from him, I hurried to the brass basin, dipping my hands into the cool water. It calmed my racing heartbeat and cooled the warm flush on my cheeks. Keeping my back to him, I took deep breaths and reminded myself of who I was and why I'd come. This was only the beginning. I'd win. Eventually.

26

Kedron Abbadon escorted me back to my chambers within the castle, promising to show me more later. He kissed my hands as he left me, and when my fingers grazed his wrists, I felt the pulse of his heartbeat thundering in anticipation. When I closed the door and was alone again, finally, I wondered if he was as nervous as I was. Except for a different reason. He'd had years to think this through, to plot and plan, all the while searching for me. While I'd just grown accustomed to him. Suddenly, it was all too much. My vision tunnel and my legs gave way. I slide to the floor and pressed my palm to my mouth while my limbs shook uncontrollably. I let it come, as Donia had instructed me in the Meditation Meadows.

When you are overwhelmed by your emotions, you need to sit down and take a deep breath. We can only hold back our emotions for so long until they build inside us, like a poison spreading throughout our bodies. Eventually, it will overwhelm us, like the waters of the river. When it rains it fills, but the water does not stay stagnate, it continues to flow and balances out again. We need to do the same. Let your feelings flow out and feel your fears and anger and sadness and hope. Do not act upon it, but feel it all until the sensation of overwhelm goes away and you are in control once again.

Tears streamed down my cheeks, and even though it had been my choice to come here, to take a dark and devious path to destroy the angel of death, I felt very much alone. I had no information, no news of what was happening beyond the castle, outside of the capital. Had Adomos found a way in after they escorted him out? Would Kedron recall his warriors from harassing the defenders? My thoughts flickered to Takari, far from the haven of Anon Loam, with no one to escort her back. If I caused chaos in the capital, would allies come to fight? Would the centaurs leave their woods and the elves travel through the mists to wage war? Or would I be alone? Again.

When the tears ceased, I wiped my face, kicked off the uncomfortable shoes, and paced. The doors to the balcony were locked, but that did not keep me from looking out over the city. I had a view of the front of the castle, the towers below, and the bridge where guards marched a steady flow back and forth. I watched them for a while, the surety of what they did and the steadiness of their movements. Each had a place where they belonged and they carried out their tasks without question. Surely I could learn a lesson from them.

Hesitations about my upcoming wedding fled as I considered what I needed to do next. In Anon Loam, the sword had been hidden in the treasury, and I assumed Kedron would have one too. Perhaps a private treasury where his possessions were kept. All I needed to do was find it. For as he'd said, the sword was mine.

Sitting down on the bed, I crossed my legs and took deep breaths. Using my senses, I felt my magic deep within and used it to reach out, searching for the sword and any other connections within the castle. With my eyes closed, I traveled through stone halls, around dark corners, and into narrow passageways. Searching, searching. There. An inkling came, a faint pulse or heartbeat, from somewhere far below me. Holding onto the thread, I stilled myself further, barely daring to breathe. The sword was here, hidden in the belly of the castle.

In my mind, I traced the steps to find it, holding tight to the memory. Footsteps echoed past my room, disturbing my flow, and I lost it. With a sigh, I sat up straight and rolled back my shoulders. Enough. I'd found it. Now I needed the chance to slip away and take it up again. I silently debated.

Tonight was the announcement, and soon servants would come to prepare me for this evening. Unfamiliar with the tradition of the castle, I could not imagine what they'd do to prepare me for the evening. Aside from changing my dress and providing more of the uncomfortable shoes that chaffed my feet. The sun was low in the sky, and I doubted I'd have an opportunity to sneak away before they came for me. So I waited, meditating to calm myself.

THEY CAME BEFORE SUNDOWN, Lady Enyd, and her silent servants. This time, they arrived armed with supplies. They filled the room with shoes and clothing, jewelry and books, parchment and ink. Stunned, I watched, and the knowledge of who I was and what was happening sank in. They moved around me as though I were already the crowned queen, expressions blank, eyes cast down to avoid looking at me. Here, there was no friendship, and yet I couldn't help but want a signal, a sign that I wasn't alone. Adomos had warned me of this.

My evening gown was a dress of pale pink, a depiction of youth and beauty. A long train dragged behind my legs while it was shorter in the front, leaving my ankles bare. Once again, it dipped in the front displaying an expanse of cleavage I was not comfortable with, but I let my mind retreat far away. I was doing what needed to be done, but as I followed the servants out of the hall, I had the dark suspicion that I was selling my soul in exchange for others' freedom.

The banquet hall had rows upon rows of tables, all full of people. Wide-eyed, I stared, taking in their brightly colored clothing, painted faces, and the amount of skin they blatantly displayed.

Lady Enyd planted herself in front of me, blocking the view. Instead of watching, I listened to the people speak in a tongue that was harsher and sharper than my own. Some of them spoke in a deep, guttural language, but I caught snatches of words I understood.

We tarried at the entrance until Kedron Abbadon himself swept in. He rested a hand on Lady Enyd's hip and leaned so close their cheeks touched. The gesture was so familiar the hairs on my neck stood up, and a bolt of jealousy swept through me.

I pinched the soft skin of my wrist to remind myself not to react, but Kedron must have seen me flinch and his gaze rested on me. The shadows that haunted him fled, and I hadn't noticed how darkness gathered around him until he laid eyes on me. His expression changed, lips tilting up, the sharpness of his cheekbones relaxing. My doubts fled. It was clear he only had eyes for me, and while I shouldn't like that knowledge, the feeling of being wanted left me breathless with power.

He finished whispering words into Lady Enyd's ear before moving past her to me. Moving closer, he bent his head, his velvet whisper sending shivers down my spine. "Was that a hint of envy I saw on your face? I thought you did not care for me, and yet this emotion you display gives me hope."

I swallowed hard, warmth gathering on my cheeks as he took my hand. I fumbled for a lie. "It wasn't jealousy. I'm just nervous about tonight, the announcement, the banquet."

Taking my chin between his fingers, he forced me to look up at him. "You have nothing to fear. All those gathered here are beneath you, for you shall be their queen and all will look up to you. Come, I have much to show you."

I let him place my hand on his arm, and he led me away from the banquet hall to a flight of broad stairs. We climbed the velvet carpet up to a balcony that overlooked the hall. And when we walked out, the entire room appeared below me, glowing with gold and silver and silk drapery. Red and black flowers adorned each table and green vines trailed alongside them, almost as though I were in an enchanted forest.

The chatter in the hall quieted as, one by one, all eyes lifted toward us. A humming began in my ears as Kedron Abbadon lifted his hand in complete control of the audience.

"Tonight we celebrate, for I have an announcement many of you have long-awaited. When I took the kingdom, I promised a day would come when I would choose a queen, but two decades have passed and now she is here. I am honored and proud to present your future queen, Princess Evie Mor.

A roar of applause coasted to my ears, and all I felt was the sensation of drowning. What had I done?

The tinkling of crystals clinking together chimed in my mind, resonating over and over again like a gong rung in warning. Voices filled my ears, but they were muddled because I could not hear correctly. The room swam with faces. Women with painted faces, bodies covered in strings of pearls and diamonds. Men with angular faces, some with horns on their heads. Others were tall, beautiful with dark skin and glistening runes on their arms. Nephilim. Just like Adomos.

Across the banquet hall, all the people of Labraid were represented. Humans, elves, ice men, fauns, nymphs, faerie, and more I did not recognize. My head swam with the knowledge of just how firm of a hold the angel of death had on Labraid, and how I could possibly believe killing him would make a difference. Him. The one who held my hand. Who presented me as lords and ladies and representatives of other nobilities congratulated me, no, us, on our upcoming wedding. A wedding which would never take place if I could help it.

I responded woodenly to each introduction, repeating words I did not mean. All the while I felt his gaze on me, studying me, capturing each word that came out of my mouth and studying it for later. My stomach fluttered, and I nibbled at the plate of food step before me, focusing on the drink to keep my nerves at bay. It only increased them.

The evening dragged on with a riot of dancing and drinking and music. Kedron Abbadon did not hover around me, but nor did he leave me alone. His dark presence was always nearby and pressure squeezed my chest. Even the calming lull of magic was nowhere to be found.

When the evening ended, I collapsed into a bed and let a deep slumber take me away from the consciousness of my predicament.

27

The days passed in an endless blur, one after the other until I lost count. Each day, I was bathed, dressed in finery, and guided through a series of encounters by Lady Enyd. I quickly learned that my position as a future queen was to give Kedron Abbadon an advantage as he negotiated with delegates from across Labraid. I was often invited to sit in the throne room and listen, wordless and beautiful, while others came before him to pay tribute or offer warriors for his army. Their actions left me curious. Why did he need an army if there was no one to fight?

Often, after leaving the throne room, the clarity of the words spoken there slipped my mind, as though the memory had been erased. I suspected my food and drink had been laced with magic. I did not feel like myself, and I wondered if he had the power to drain my magic and turn me into a shadow of what had been. Or perhaps my mother was right about the castle. It was cursed, and the longer I stayed within, the more difficult it became to breathe.

One morning, I woke to the glow of daylight and a breeze rich with the scent of bark and tree sap. The doors to the balcony had been unlocked for the first time since my stay in the castle. In a moment I was out of bed, my toes curled on the warm stones. The wind blew like a promise of hope, lifting the veil of fog from my mind and bringing me clarity.

Everything that had happened since I left the Beluar Woods felt like a lifetime ago. I was a different person now, but a sense of nostalgia made me wish I were back under the boughs of those old trees where the woes of the world could not touch me. Ironic, how I'd wanted a place to belong, and now, looking back, I realized the centaurs were my family. The reminder of why I'd left sent a bolt of determination through me.

The door to my room squeaked open, and a servant entered with a tray of food. It was the usual fare: figs, toast, eggs, and a slab of meat. Today was ham. I resolved not to eat it. Perhaps the dullness in my mind would stay gone if I did not taste the food.

The servant's eyes widened when she glimpsed me on the balcony, but she ducked her head and hurried to the washroom to draw a bath. Usually, I sat down to eat before bathing, but today I joined her, tossing off my nightclothes before setting into lavender-scented water.

Each morning I bathed, soaking in the fragrant water which caused my skin to become softer. The calluses on my hands faded and my body filled out. The hard muscle was still underneath, but I looked less like a half-starved warrior and more like a princess. Even in Anon Loam, where I'd been well fed and taken care of, I hadn't noticed a change in my appearance. Now, the servant scattered flower petals on top of the water while I leaned back, letting the water and oil do its work.

The sound of a door shutting started me and I jolted up, splashing water over the side. Eyes wide, I stared at my servant and she stared back at me, surprise making her lose her steely composure.

Heavy footsteps thumped in the room, as though the person who had entered wanted to frighten us, wanted us to know they were there. I shifted in the tub and pressed my hands over my breasts. "Shut the door," I hissed, feeling bad I didn't know the servant's name.

I wondered whether they were ordered not to speak to me, to make me feel isolated. Kedron Abbadon—my enemy—was the only one I could speak to.

The servant hastened to the door just as a shadow darkened it. I knew who it was before he spoke.

"Leave us," Kedron ordered.

My chest went tight and my eyes darted around the room as my servant hastened away, leaving me naked and vulnerable. There was no time to leap out of the tub and dress myself, and the towels were too far away to reach without exposing myself. Instead, I sank further into the tub until the waters rose to my neck.

Kedron's profile filled the doorway. He wore black, as usual. His body was hidden in a swirling cloak that fell to the floor. His pointed ears twitched as he regarded me, a sinister smile on his angular face. "Evie Mor," he said.

"Why are you here?" my voice caught in my throat, his presence intimidating me. Even though I saw him almost daily, we hadn't been alone together since we signed the contract. My resolve to be bold dissolved under the magnetic power of his presence.

"It is time," he announced, gliding closer until he stood over the waters.

I trembled at his proximity and tried to shrink away. "Please, let me dress, and then we will speak."

His lips parted, revealing a flash of teeth. "On the contrary, I enjoy seeing you like this."

I dipped my chin, desperately searching for a way out. He wanted to see me weak and willing. All this time, he'd subtly been trying to destroy my self-awareness and courage. If I listened to him, would he go away? But no, he perched on the edge of the tub, in danger of falling in. Tapping his long fingers on the side where droplets of water hung, he studied me. "You've been here for over a month now. How is the castle to your liking?"

The scent of mint leaves and grapefruit was stronger than the bath oils. I swallowed hard and focused on a spot on the wall where a speck of mold spread. "You already know what I think, and yet you bait me with your words. Speak plainly. What is it time for?"

"You don't sound like a queen who is excited about her upcoming wedding."

"I. . ." I opened my mouth and closed it, fumbling and failing to find an excuse.

All the while, his fingers moved closer to me,

sliding down the edge of the tub to play in the waters.

"If you must know, I do not look forward to that day." I could not bring myself to say the word *wedding*, as I shrank away from his searching hand.

"No, I would assume not, even though you signed a blood contract."

I bit my lower lip, unable to keep my eyes on the spot of mold as I watched him graze a petal and toss it away.

"I will uphold my end of the contract," my words whistled out from between my teeth as his fingers wrapped around the ends of my hair.

"You signed with blood and have no choice but to uphold it. But the walls of the castle must be unusual for you, one born and raised in the forest. How odd it must be to succumb to the whims of the people, to be bathed and dressed by servants, and served rich food on platters. It is not what you were born to do, is it?"

The truth of his words wormed into my heart and I met his gaze, finding unexpected sympathy in the orbs of his black eyes. "Aye." My shoulders slumped. "It is true."

"You want to be more than a queen, sitting on a throne and ruling over others, don't you?"

His tone sank down, softly lulling me, unraveling

the hard places where I sought to keep him out. The most frustrating part was how he understood me, fully, as though he'd walked beside me my entire life and knew my insecurities and desires. It would be so easy to just let go of who others thought I was and my purpose as a child of the gods, a warrior princess meant to bring down the rule of a clever angel.

When his hand cupped my cheek turning me to face him, I let him. Suddenly, I was so tired of searching for a place to belong, fighting to right the wrongs of the world, and ending up alone and misunderstood. Tilting my head, I moved as though I had no control over myself, magic fluttering in my belly. A gray haze surrounded us and I trailed a wet finger over his sharp cheekbones down to his neck. Clasping my fingers around the base of his neck, I pulled him closer and initiated the kiss.

It was long and seductive, and when he parted my lips with his tongue, I let him. Somewhere within me came the cry that this was wrong, yet the deliciousness of the kiss left me feeling lightheaded. My embarrassment faded away but only for a moment. He pulled back, jaw tight, eyes dark, and stood. Taking a towel, he held it open and waited.

I hesitated, fingers clutching the rim of the tub as I lifted myself out and stood before him. Water streamed down my body, pooling on the floor as Kedron kneeled in front of me. He started at my feet, drying me off slowly, taking his time, and forcing my legs further apart. My stomach dipped and fluttered as he caressed my skin then lifted my leg over his shoulder, opening my core to him.

I sucked in a deep breath, resting my fingers on his shoulder for balance. So this was how it would happen. This was how he'd take me, claim me, ruin me. Without a word, he put down the towel and moved his hands up my thighs. My skin tingled as his tongue flickered out, sending waves of ecstasy through my body. It was like nothing I'd expected, and a thousand sensations fired through me. This was what I wanted to feel; the heights of pleasure were so intense it left my limbs boneless. My head lulled back, and I closed my eyes, letting everything drop away except for the present moment.

28

Afterward, he washed the blood from my legs and helped me dress in a gown the color of the sky. I wanted to lie down and rest, to sleep, and let the pleasure and pain soak through me. But he gently pulled me from the bed and held me against his lean body. "No, there is something I want you to see."

"Now?" the words did not feel like mine, and in the haze of passion, I knew he had utterly seduced me.

He chuckled. "It is still early morning. The time to rest will come later."

I didn't think I could walk in heels, not after what he'd done to me, but he found slippers to cushion my feet and wrapping an arm around my waist escorted me from the room.

I blinked against the low light as we left, and as my vision adjusted, I realized guards stood outside my door, not one, but two on either side dressed in full armor. My face warmed and I wondered whether they'd heard what happened behind closed doors, but they did not look in our direction as we passed. Kedron held me close to him, and I had some time to unravel my thoughts as we walked. Something had changed during the last hour we'd spent together, but I could not put a finger on exactly what had changed. I needed some time alone to think.

It wasn't until we followed a series of passageways and stairs down into the depths of darkness that I realized the truth. Being with him, near him, touching him, tasting him had brought me to the realization that perhaps all this time, I hadn't been waiting to slay my enemy. I'd been searching for my lover. Someone like me; who completed me in every way. I turned that consideration over in my mind. He was old and immortal. But I would be too, and after decades I'd consider age to be insignificant and only see the potential of the future. Just like him.

Could I be his dark queen? He claimed he had recalled his elites to the capital, and aside from lesser demons, the lands of Labraid were free from his squads. If I trusted him, and he trusted me, we could shape the future of Labraid together. I'd be Queen Evie Mor. The sound of my name with the word queen before it tasted wickedly delightful. I'd take back my kingdom, but not in the way my mother had wanted or what my younger sister, Brianna, hoped for. I'd take it my way and rule surrounded by wealth and power and magic and. . .love. If Kedron Abbadon was capable of love. After what had happened in the room, it felt like he cared for me. Even though he'd been demanding and persistent, he'd also been gentle. I did not detect a lie in his kiss, his touch, and I thirsted for more.

Kedron released me and pulled a key out of his pocket. I hadn't been paying attention to our journey, and now I stepped back, feeling stronger, and examined the area. A single torch lit the dark passageway, and we stood at the end, a heavy door in front of us. Kedron put the key in the lock and it turned slowly, straining and squeaking as though trying to prevent us from entering.

Dampness hung in the air, and I hugged my arms around myself, chilled by the lack of clothing. The warmth of summer was banished here in the depths of the castle, and I wished I had a cloak like the one Kedron wore. "What is this place?" I whispered, my voice shaking as I shivered.

"This is the secret of the capital city." The lock gave with a screech and Kedron pushed his shoulder against the door. It moved slowly as though resistant to him. "You spent some time with the queen of men, did you not?"

A heaviness descended on my shoulders. "I did."

He caught my eye, his voice soft. "I heard she was killed. I'm sorry."

I froze, staring at him. I was already losing myself, my soul, to him, and he didn't make it any easier. He was supposed to be evil, a killer, the angel of death, and yet, those two words, "I'm sorry," would be my undoing. My jaw went tight because it was supposed to be his fault. He'd driven the king and queen away from the capital and had indirectly caused their demise. Briefly, I wondered what had happened to the king because Brianna hadn't told me.

"Did she tell you about this place?" Kedron prodded.

"No." I shook my head, recalling how angry I'd been at her deception. Had my father seduced her the way Kedron seduced me? I swallowed hard. Perhaps I was more like her than I cared to be.

He took my hand and pulled me into the entrance of the chamber. Stones rose above and a staircase spiraled down into the depths of obscurity.

An uneasiness settled around me, and I involuntarily took a step closer to him. Under the layer of mustiness was another smell almost like fire but not quite. Something was wrong down there, and I didn't want to find out what. But Kedron did not give me a choice. He led us to the stairs and spoke as we descended.

"This is the treasure of the capital. The gated chamber between this world and the world below. Long ago, the gods warred, and the result was the banishment of fallen angels to the underworld. Banished from the light, the darkness deformed them until they became known as demons, a terror to look upon. Misunderstood and hated, they became a scourge. And when they go free, they cause chaos throughout the land. But it doesn't have to be that way. A new era is coming when gods and angels and demons will dwell together in one world, and all people will have the chance to live life as they please. This world, Labraid, has always belonged to those with long life, the immortals. It did before the war, and it shall again. My goal has been to restore Labraid to the way it was before when gods walked among us and the land was ripe with magic. Demons were not a scourge, simply those who lived by moonlight. The kingdom of men was built to guard the gates and keep them from opening. But the time has come for us to usher in a new era. The king and queen of men are gone, and you and I are not human. How fitting is it to start our kingdom afresh, anew, with the rise of the fallen, an immortal kingdom that shall live on, long after the history of the kingdom of men has been forgotten?"

My breath came short and fast with each word he spoke, unraveling the dream I'd held earlier when we walked the halls of the castle in the light. Down in the very foundations of the castle, where water leaked in and a dull, green light pulsed, the truth rose before me. Kedron Abbadon was the angel of death, the embodiment of evil, and I'd been seduced by him. It was likely that he'd counted on my youth and innocence in his elaborate plan to make me his dark queen and tempt me into opening the gates to the underworld. It all became clear. This was what Adomos had warned me about. Kedron wanted me for a reason, and I'd just discovered what it was.

I opened my mouth to speak, but words gathered like ash in my dry throat. Besides, it was too late. We'd reached the bottom of the stairs in a circular chamber. In the middle was a circle with symbols carved into stone, like a compass. Deep grooves in the stone held a bit of water and my stomach turned. Out of the floor came the green light, pulsing as though beneath us was something else, concealed by the weight of the stone.

Pressing my free hand against my heart, I shook my head. "I can't. . .we can't do this."

Kedron whirled to face me at once, taking both my hands in his. "We can and we will. Do you know how long I've waited for you? To complete the mission? The ultimate quest to do what none has ever done before."

Tears rose, and I fought to keep them down, my voice shaking. "Why?"

His eyes bored into mine. "You've seen this world, haven't you? Although you haven't walked from end to end, you've seen the way the gods have forsaken it. They boast of great magic and power, but when the people do not follow their ways, they leave them to doom and gloom. It is time the gods answered for what they have done, and the state they left the world in. I shall call forth the fallen angels of the underworld, and they will force the gods to reckon with this world. There will come a war like none have seen before. But it is much more than that. It is a cleansing of the old ways and ushering in a new era of Labraid. I invite you to rule with me because together nothing will stop us. I'm not like those of your past, who want you to free them from supposed oppression or use you because of your magic and royal blood. Think, did I force you to come with me? Did I ask you to do anything against your will? Even earlier today, you initiated what happened between us. Right now, I'm giving you everything you ever wanted, making your wildest dreams come true. This is what you want."

But it wasn't a question. Merely a statement, telling me, forcing me to see the world from his perspective. The problem was that tiny bits of truth floated in his words, laced with a poison that was difficult to unravel. Closing my eyes, I rested my head on his chest, my entire body trembling. What he offered me was more than anyone else had offered, and yet it would mean compromising my mission to kill him. Except the knowledge lay heavy on my chest that even though he proposed something terrible that would have drastic effects across the world, I did not want to kill him. Not anymore.

"I. . . I can't."

"Can't or won't?"

"Won't," my voice died away into a whisper. I expected him to react, to throw me against the wall and force me against my will, but the silence was even more frightening.

Letting go of his cloak, I stepped away and willed the magic within me to rise. It was slow to come, unused for so long, and my hands shook as the cold air of the chamber made my skin tingle. Kedron watched me out of lidded eyes, and then he pounced. Just as before, he was quick, faster than I imagined. A knife plunged into my side and a scream burst out of my throat. Forgetting about my magic, I used my hands to staunch the flow as he removed the blade, cut through his own arm, and then plunged it into the center of the compass-like circle.

Two things entered my mind at once. It was blood. All this time he'd needed my blood and while the wound hurt, it wasn't deep nor life-threatening. Secondly, it was too late to resist. The ground trembled.

Kedron stood stall, a glint of triumph in the orbs of eyes, even more soulless now. He spread his arms, letting the blood stain his cloak. "It is done."

It was my moment. If I had the red sword, I could have run him through while he stood there, basking in his success. Instead, I slumped to my knees, a sob building inside. I had failed. Failed to take the kingdom of men. Failed to save Labraid from demons. Failed to bring freedom to the oppressed. It was over, and he had won.

29

The stones shook beneath me as I clutched my side to stanch the flow of blood and leaned against the wall for support. Kedron stepped back from the center of the circle as cracks formed on the dip grooves and blinding green light streamed out. I closed my eyes, unable to look at it, and a moment later, two arms lifted me up.

Kedron cradled me against his chest as he carried me up the flight of stairs. "I will take you to a healer, but first you must see what happens next."

I didn't respond, couldn't, as my emotions overwhelmed me. Instead of rising strong, I'd allowed myself to be seduced by a liar, a dark angel set on destroying the world to gain a new foothold, new land for himself. No, for the immortals, angels, demons, gods, and Nephilim. My side burned where he'd pierced me, and I wanted what he'd done to be a lie because of earlier today. How he'd made love to me had felt real. Now, this.

"Look," Kedron commanded, setting me down gently on a rock.

Mist sprayed my face, and when I opened my eyes, my pain faded away, forgotten under the beauty that lay before me. We'd left the castle and come out on the rocks which overlooked the great ocean. Behind us towered the castle and more craggy rocks covered with moss and seaweed and crustaceans. It was beautiful out there. The air was tangy and crisp. The rays of sunlight warm after the chill of the hidden chamber. The ground did not shake and what had happened seemed like nothing more than a nightmare.

Choppy waves splashed upon the rocky shore, leaving what looked like soapy suds as it rushed out again. A heavy mist hung in the distance, but even beyond that, rocks rose out of the waters, great boulders for ships to crash upon.

I breathed in the salty air and peeled my bloody hand away from my side. I'd seen bodies of water, but nothing as enormous and powerful as this. "You would destroy the beauty of Labraid because you can."

"No." Kedron remained standing beside it, staring out at the ocean. "I would see a new world ushered in. One where those like us don't have to hide. A world where we can use our magic freely without armies to protect us from those who would seek to slay us. You've seen how the gods and goddesses act, haven't you? You know what it's like to be desired for your blood, tortured because of who you are. The odds are stacked against us from the beginning and those who die, those with short lives, use us and take everything from us. It should not be this way. The world belongs to those with power, as it was from the beginning, so shall it be now."

"But you're wrong," I protested, unable to explain why, but because everything within my gut warned me against his words. "You act like you're a god, as though you can determine the way of the world. It is not for you to decide."

"Is it not? Have you seen what I've done? I've wrenched control of the kingdom away from humans. I've lured you to my kingdom, to be my queen and rule alongside me. Yet you doubt me. It is not your fault."

His words were gentle, and he sat down beside me, sliding an arm around my shoulders, although I stiffened at his touch. That was the problem. His very touch made me long for him, and yet his words created a distance between us. Knowing what he believed, I could never offer myself up to him, nor allow the trajectory of his future goals to continue. But my heart wanted to give up and give in because this was the closest I'd come to finding where I belonged. And what he offered me was more than any other had given me. He recognized my royal identity and wanted me to rule by his side. I doubted my mother had intended me to rule. After my conversation with Brianna, I knew she was the one who'd rule while I'd stand by her side as a guard. That was not the life I wanted for myself.

"You were raised to believe in the old gods, to pray to them, and use their wisdom to guide your life. Especially in the Beluar Woods, there's a reason no one goes there to contest with the will of the centaurs. Their faith is strong. They will fight to the death against anyone who opposes them, and that is the danger of placing your belief in the wrong gods. Do you firmly believe the gods care about them and their faithfulness?"

"I do," I said. "I've seen what their faith does for them."

"And what did their faith do for you? Were you not left alone, forsaken by your birth mother and father? Did they travel with you into the kingdom of men or leave you on your own?"

I pressed my lips together, unable to answer his question. My thoughts fled back to the ritual that had taken place after I'd ascended the hill of the gods to ask for guidance. I'd been shown the path that led to my mother, and I believed the gods wanted me to find her and learn my purpose. I'd gone alone because it was the plan laid out from my life, to take up the red sword and free the kingdom of men from the angel of death. But what if I, too, had free will to make my own decisions and what the gods offered me was only a suggestion? I still had the choice to choose my destiny.

"They taught me all they could," I protested in their defense. "I left with a guide, but when I entered the Vale of Monsters, Jezebel captured me." Bitterness rang out as the name of the goddess passed through my lips.

"Did you not question the gods and ask them if that was what they intended for your life?"

"I did. When she captured me the second time. I prayed for my father to save me, but he never came."

"No. Don't you see? The gods have forsaken this world, they don't care what happens. If you want to hear from them, to force them into action, you must call upon those they hate most. It takes a significant act for the gods to pay attention to this land again, and if the greater demons from the underworld are invited into our realm, they will wage war. This land will be cleansed and a new era will come. The old gods, the ones who did not care, will be banished, perhaps locked in the very underworld where they banished the fallen angels. And a new kingdom will come, our kingdom. Tell me, Evie Mor, do you care what happens to the inhabitants of Labraid?"

"I do," I whispered. A weakness came over me because I knew where his question was leading and I did not know how to fight him.

"Because you care, you will make a better queen than those who came before you, and because you have the blood of the gods, your immortal reign shall continue until the end of days."

I stared at him because part of me wanted to believe him. His words made sense. "What about you? What makes you hate the gods and why do you propose this new kingdom when you caused so much death? You ripped away the kingdom of men without remorse."

"The kingdom of men was corrupt. Someone needed to step in and halt the chaos. I was the only one with the power to do so."

I closed my eyes briefly, recalling what my

mother had said about the kingdom of men, and Romulus' words about how corrupt it was. So much so, the defenders rose to stand against the kingdom of men. Kedron was right, something had to change, but was his way right? Did there have to be a ruler or was it possible for the people to rule themselves, to build relationships without standing under the rule of a king or queen? But who would watch over the world and protect it? As much as I wanted to fight Kedron, it was easy to believe the words, whether they were, indeed, truths or lies.

Still, I held firm to the fact that opening the underworld was a drastic action and the wrong way to bring down the gods. Many innocents would be caught in the war and many would die. Yet he seemed to relish it, leaving me with the speculation that something had happened in his past. Something that made him want to war against the gods, and I, with my royal blood, was the ideal accomplice to his plans.

Rubbing my bloody hand on my dress—because it was already ruined—I forced myself to look Kedron in the eye. "You're saying that we are the ones who must judge the gods?"

"You catch on quickly." A note of approval rang in his tone.

Facing the rough waters again, I considered the

goddess, Jezebel. Were there more like her who had been cast down and sought to corrupt the world in return for vengeance? Had I fallen from her snare only to land in that of Kedron Abbadon? I repeated my earlier question. "What happened in your past? Why are you against the gods?"

"It is a long tale I do not wish to repeat." He took my hand. "Time is limited right now, and I must take you to a healer. You must understand. What I did back there was to move our plan forward. Time had delayed me for a long time, but no more. I brought you out here for a reason, hoping you might come to understand the world from my perspective. I know it much to ask, and you do not have decades of experience as I do. But it will come, if only you take a leap of faith, and trust me."

I squeezed his hand, but not in understanding. It was ironic he used the words faith and trust, something I'd hoped our earlier tryst would seal.

"Beyond the land of Labraid are the waters of the great ocean, and at the very bottom in the depths is a door. We unlocked the gates and now the door will open and they will come across the great waters to fight for us."

"They are demons. How can you control them?"

"Ah. You don't know how important you are, do you? What do you know of Claíomh Dearg?"

"The Red Sword," I clarified. "It's the sword of a destroyer and, according to legend, it is used to defeat demons."

Kedron flashed his teeth, a bemused expression crossing his face. "Aye, the sword of the destroyer. And do you know why it defeats demons?"

"No," I whispered.

"Because the red sword controls them. When the demons come, they will swear allegiance to whoever carries the red sword, and right now, that is you."

The trembling began in my toes until my entire body shook as though I shivered from a great cold. Even my teeth chattered as I spoke. "That can't be possible."

"Aye, it is possible. Think about it. The sword of the destroyer forged at the very same time the gates were locked. The gods held that if anyone should unlock the gates of the underworld, someone had to control the swarms that would come forth, and they would belong to the keeper of the red sword. That is the reason none have been able to control it. The power is too great; power that should only belong to a god. Or goddess. Like you, my future queen."

"No," I shook my head, my voice but was a whisper as the truth sank in. Still, I wanted to deny it.

Kedron continued as if guessing what I would

ask next. "The blade was here when I stormed the capital city, ready to take it as my own, but the king and queen of men fled with it. I sent my armies to recover it but they were too late. When I next heard of the sword, it had been secreted into the elven haven of Anon Loam and willed to you. It was only later, when I learned the truth about your birth, that the brilliance of the deception became clear."

I whimpered, but he went on as though he hadn't heard me.

"Your father is the god Dagda, a warrior who fights demons and other supernatural beings, and his magic carries the power of life and death. So you see, you were born with a purpose. To take up the red sword and continue the work of your father. To fight against demons and other beings who invade this world. You and the sword will lead us to victory, as we war against the gods."

30

I must have passed out because when I opened my eyes I lay in bed. A tiny woman stood over me, white hair pulled back in a bun, her cheeks sagging with wrinkles. Her bright blue eyes were sharp with a hint of tiredness as she patted my side where the knife wound was. I glanced down, making out the bandage around my waist. It didn't hurt anymore and my hands were free of blood.

"Oh," the woman exclaimed, pressing a hand to her heart. Her eyes darted around the room as if someone had heard her then she leaned forward. "You'll be better in no time. In fact, your wound was already healing."

Blood of the gods, which ensured I healed

quickly without scars, but I did not tell her that. "You must be a healer," I said instead. "Thank you."

"You look just like her, you know," she said in a friendly whisper. "Except your hair is red instead of black."

I stiffened as her words sank in. "You knew my mother, Queen Ceana Mor?"

"That I did." She sighed, a painful smile crossing her face. "She wasn't happy here. I hope wherever she ended up, she's much happier."

Questions flooded my mind. Why didn't she flee with my mother? Was she a friend come to make me feel comfortable? Or a foe who'd later report what I'd said to Kedron?

"She was," I confirmed.

The woman patted my arm. "It is a boon to hear good news from outside of the capital. We all feared when the angel of death came to reign, but what choice did we have but to follow him?" Suddenly she pressed her hands over her mouth, eyes wide with alarm. "I say all of this in front of the queen to be, please, forgive my tongue. It slipped."

"I will not repeat anything you say here to anyone else," I confirmed.

The woman remained standing still as tears filled her blue eyes. "Forgive the ramblings of an old woman. It's just that you look so much like her in her youth, and they always said the prophecy would come true. I didn't believe it was possible, but here you are."

I propped myself up on one elbow, wincing with the effort. "What prophecy?"

"Oh you know," the woman waved her hands, "the one about a new kingdom, a new land where all the old will be washed away and a new kingdom will rise, ruled by one who is kind and gentle without a hint of corruption."

I stared at her. "I've never heard of that prophecy."

"Oh." She wiped at her eyes. "It's kept in the old scrolls in the library, under lock and key. Hardly anyone knows about them."

With a sigh, she sat down on the edge of my bed and placed vials and bandages into a bag. "I'm Moli, the castle healer. I've been working with herbs and potions longer than I can remember. When the castle was taken, well, I hid in my room until it was all over, and then they found a use for me. I've been here ever since, and I admit, I thought I'd be beheaded along with the rest, but I was granted mercy. When your mother was here, the old scrolls weren't locked up, and she often read over them.

Curious words and old texts, I don't know if she believed in them or not, yet they seem to be coming true."

I barely dared to breathe, hesitant to break her train of thought. "Who wrote the scrolls?"

"An ancient scholar is credited with being responsible for the scrolls. He traveled the world and penned the first account of Labraid, the inhabitants, and what was to come. Many said he had the ear of the gods and that was why some of his words were called prophetic. Other rumors said he was one of the ice men, which is even more curious since they were here the night the capital fell. If not for the angel of death, many would have blamed the ice men for destroying the peace we had here. Ah, here I go again, unable to hold my tongue. Listen, I should not be speaking to you, you have a wedding coming up soon and should heal and rest." She squinted. "Although if what they say about you is true, you will be healed overnight."

I pondered her words as she rose, and before she reached the door, the question burst out of my lips. "In the prophecies, is there a mention of the red sword?"

Moli narrowed her brows in confusion.

"Claíomh Dearg," I clarified.

Her face went pale, and she shook her head.

"That is an evil sword. Best to stay away from it. I told your mother not to take it, but she did, against my wisdom. It's probably for the best that it's lost now. No one should touch it."

So she didn't know where it was, nor that it was in the palace. I nodded at her, both in appreciation and dismissal. She'd given me something to think about, but more than anything I had to weigh the words Kedron Abbadon had spoken, about the new kingdom, the reign of gods, and controlling the demons.

Alone once more, I forced myself out of bed, ignoring the faint throb of my wound. Dressing, I paced back and forth while the evening hues blazed across the night sky. Kedron's words and actions meant I had to act, and quickly. Now that I was away from him and his seductive presence, my mind felt clear, like my own again, and I could think and consider what I personally wanted.

First, I had to find the red sword.

Second, I needed to know how long I had until the greater demons would come ashore. Kedron had made it sound like they had to ascend from the depths of the ocean, which might only take a matter of days. I had to assume time was short and if I didn't act, the world would be doomed.

Sitting on the edge of a chair, I dropped my head

into my hands and massaged my forehead. Guilt rose like a choking wave. This was my fault too, wasn't it? I'd come to Kedron Abaddon of my own free will, and now I'd allowed him to enact his master plan. It was like freeing the goddess Jezebel, but on a much large, world-ending scale.

I stayed that way for a long time, taking deep breaths, slowing my heart rate and meditating on what I must do. According to Moli, the wedding ceremony would be soon and then, officially, I'd be queen. His queen. I thought of the blood contract and wondered how important it was that I fulfilled my end of the contract before causing chaos. But whatever happened, I needed to be ready. It was better that I do as much as possible before becoming queen, and while my mind was clear. In Kedron's presence, my strength and will ebb away because he filled that secret longing, one I'd had my entire life. I wanted to belong somewhere, and not just fit in, but to be wanted, desired for who I was, and he had shown me what love looked like. Far beyond what Adomos had given me.

I touched my fingers to my lips, a sudden hunger rising within, for his touch, his taste. No matter what kind of magic he was using on me, I could not be weak. I was a daughter of a god. Closing my fingers into fists, I rose, pulled on a pair of slippers, and went to the door. My fingers trembled on the knob, but it turned. My shoulders sagged in relief. I wasn't locked in. But as I opened it, my gaze was drawn up to the guard standing on the threshold.

31

My door was guarded day and night by one, sometimes two, guards. I'd grown to ignore them as I came and went with my servants, always to somewhere in the castle to meet with Kedron Abbadon. Tonight, I'd forgotten, and surprise covered my face. I took a step back as the guard lifted an armored hand to his helm, lifting the visor enough to show me his face. He pressed his other hand to his lips and my alarm increased.

Familiar golden eyes met mine as he uncurled a fist and held out a piece of parchment. I dared not say his name aloud, and yet my heart skipped a beat. Adomos was here. He hadn't failed at all and had managed to become one of my guards. I wasn't alone. The relief of that knowledge threatened to bend me in half, and a rush of tears came to my eyes. I blinked hard to keep them from brimming over and forced myself not to leap into his arms. Instead, I took the paper and unfolded it.

"Keep your gaze away from mine," Adomos said in his low voice. "This passage leads to the king's hall of treasures. That is where you'll find the sword."

"Thank you," I whispered.

Even though it felt wrong to walk away, I padded down the hall, head down. When I reached an alcove, I slipped into it and held the parchment up to the torchlight. Markings on one side showed where my doorway must be, and then a path that led down a twisted maze of halls and staircases. I squared my shoulders, memorizing as much as I could. If I walked with purpose, head down, perhaps no one would recognize me, even with my flaming red hair. I did not have a cloak in my room to cover my head, but I was supposed to be sleeping off my wound.

The castle was far from quiet at night, and I guessed it was nearing the dinner hour. Nobles in their finery moved past me, not sparing a glance in my direction. Eventually, the halls quieted down, and aside from a few people here and there, I was mostly alone. I couldn't forget about the guards and had to assume the treasury would be guarded. In Anon Loam, I'd entered from the outside, making it easy to take the sword, but here it would be impossible unless I fought my way in.

My footsteps slowed as I approached the entrance to a wide hall. On either side rose carvings of great kings of men, towering fifteen feet above me, their toes almost as big as my hands. An aura of sacredness hung in the air and goosebumps pebbled on my arms. Here, hidden things remained under lock and key, and I wondered if it also included the ancient scrolls.

Ducking behind a pillar, I studied the hall, which was bathed in shadows. The heavy clang of footsteps moving back and forth rang out. Sure enough, on the other side of the expanse marched a solitary guard in front of a massive door. The symbol of a lion glinted on it, with the lock in its mouth. An intimidating display of power. Sticking my tongue in my cheek, I considered my options. It was not likely the guard had the key, and my stomach soured as I realized who did. Kedron. I hadn't been to his bedchamber, but I guessed it would be there, or on his person. Earlier, when he had disrobed, I hadn't seen a key, but nor had I seen the blade he stabbed me with.

Crossing my arms, I leaned against the pillar.

One guard marched in front of the doors and, by all appearances, bored, as if he didn't belong there. Why only one? I recalled the treasure in Anon Loam, guarded by magic. Closing my eyes, I used my senses to search for magic in the room. Only a faint inkling came, and whatever it was came from behind those doors, my spirit syncing with the will of the red sword.

The scent of mint and moss drifted to my nose, breaking my concentration. The whisper of a shadow came and then I knew, without looking. I felt him in every fiber of my being. Kedron Abbadon was here. He crossed to the door of the treasury, dismissing the guard with a flick of his hand. Spellbound, I waited for him to pull out the key or chant a spell to dislodge the door. He did neither. Instead, he rolled up his sleeve and pressed his arm against the lion's mouth.

I squinted in the low light, my breath coming faster as I slowly realized what he was doing. Blood. It was blood magic that unlocked the doors. Sure enough, the lion split in half and the doors opened, just enough for Kedron Abbadon to slip through. Now that I knew the secret of the door, I had to wait until he left to enter.

A wave of tiredness passed over me as I recalled I hadn't eaten all day. Careful not to make a sound, I sank to the floor, leaning against a pillar to remain hidden. I just barely had a view of the doors, but my senses were alerted to him. I'd know when he passed.

The shadows lengthened as I waited, and then came a click. Brushing sleep out of my eyes, I stood, stretching my legs, which had gone to sleep while I waited. Suppressing a yawn, I watched for Kedron to appear out of the shadows, but he did not come. Had I missed his passing? The lights in the hall burned low, adding an aura of spookiness to the sacred aura. I should not be here and yet I could not walk away and leave the world to its folly.

After another moment, I made my way across the stone, sticking close to the columns in case the guard returned. Perhaps there was another way out because the guard hadn't passed by me after he was excused. Putting it out of my mind, I approached the doors. The octane of magic was stronger, making me want to flee. Instead, I lifted my hand, scrapping my palm against the intricate design of the lion's mouth until I drew blood. Hoping it was enough, I pressed it against the keyhole and waited.

The doors gave way with a shudder, cracking open just enough to let me slip inside. Within, light flared out and gold dust glittered from above, casting a spell of radiance on the pile of treasures.

The inner chamber was a dome, filled with gold, silver, statues made of alabaster or marble, jars full of fragrant oil, strings of diamonds and pearls and crowns, in all shapes and sizes and colors. But my gaze was riveted to the very center of the room where the red sword lay on a pedestal, its voice calling, begging me to take it up. It whispered around me, an intoxication I could not ignore.

I walked toward it, maneuvering around the piles of treasure. My heart beat sped up as I reached for it. Was it true about the sword? As its keeper, was I the one who controlled demons? Could I send them back into the pit whence they'd come? If so, all was not lost.

"So, you have chosen the sword."

The low purr of Kedron's voice drifted to my ears.

I snatched my hand back and spun around, eyes widening as he stared back at me, a dangerous look crossing his face.

"You don't trust me. You wish to strike me down and rule in my place, even though I offered you the world."

I swallowed hard. Literally, he'd offered me a place at his side in the new kingdom to come, and I knew what my actions looked like. All I had to do was reach out, take up the sword, and drive it through his heart. So why did I hesitate? Why did I crave his approval?

"I'm disappointed in you, although I am not surprised. Your past continues to rule your heart. You still believe in the centaurs and the old gods. Even though I've done everything in my power to show you, it is not the way."

"You have called demons into this world by unlocking the gates of the underworld, and that I cannot forget or forgive." My words rang out strong, much bolder than I felt.

Kedron circled me. "And if I closed the gates to the underworld and sent them back, would you reign by my side as my queen?"

The word no should have been on my lips in a moment, instead, I paused, mouth open. This morning I'd been ready to give him everything and now. . .what he was offering dangled in front of me like forbidden fruit. I should say no, but my heart wanted me to say yes.

Kedron's gaze flickered from my hands to my face and the look of danger intensified into something predatory. "It pleases me to see your hesitation. Come, my queen. I've moved up our wedding day, but I see we have much to discuss before we are single-minded."

I shuddered as my hands fell to my side. "Does

that mean you'll change your mind and close the gates?"

In an instant, he was by my side. "You've had a long day, and so have I. Let's retire, rest and discuss tomorrow."

He was so close, in moments his fingers would curl through the loose strands of my braid and I'd lose sense of myself under his touch. Closing my eyes, I let my mind take over and guide me. I already knew he was much faster than I was and the only action I had on my side was the element of surprise. I lunged, letting magic guide me, and my finger closed on the hilt of the red sword.

A thirst for blood hummed through me as the voice of the sword rang out loud and clear in my mind. *Kill. Kill. Kill.*

32

"Not today," Kedron countered.

Regardless, I swung the sword up, not sure what I intended to do now that I had my hands on it. The echoes of its voice whispered around me and suddenly hate filled my heart. It wasn't directed at him but toward my situation. Why did I always have to deny myself, deny what I wanted to put everything, even my own life, at risk and save the world? I'd left a home I was comfortable with, found my mother only for her to be ripped away, and strived for peace, first in Anon Loam and then with myself in the wilds. But everything I set out to accomplish turned sour. Even this, and the sword, only magnetized my inadequate feelings.

"Listen to me. The day will come when it is time for you to take up the red sword. I will unlock the doors of the treasury and let you take it up yourself. But it is too soon, too dangerous. Think. You did not know the power of the sword and used it in the past without regard for its power. You fed it with the blood of a goddess. It is, indeed, the sword of a slayer, the sword of a monster, and you will become what you seek to destroy if you do not use it properly. Perhaps you were warned about the sword, perhaps not, but regardless, I believe you have the strength to use it. I believe in you. But the time is not now. Wait. Just a little longer, and you can fuel your anger into it, and use it."

"No," I cried. "You are the darkness that plagues this land, and with you gone, everything will return as it should be."

"Listen to yourself, as it should be. Do you know what the way of the world should be? Two decades you've walked this land. How arrogant for you to assume you know how it should be. Slay me now if you will. It's what you've wanted since you figured out who I am, isn't it?" The hurt and disappointment in his voice were scathing, but he continued. "Figure out how to close the gates yourself, princess."

I wavered because he was right. I didn't know how to shut the gates, but I knew how to enter the treasury and I could do so again. Slowly, the sword came down as my face crumbled. A wave of hunger and weakness passed over me as the sword slipped from my fingers and clattered on the floor. The voice that had been so controlling went silent while Kedron lifted me as though I weighed nothing.

"You have to do better than this, be better than this if you wish to be my queen," he scolded.

But I was too exhausted to fear him and he took me away, not back to my room where Adomos waited outside, guarding, waiting, hoping I'd succeeded. I'd dragged him into this, and now it was clear, I had no business trying to save the kingdom of men or Labraid. I was nothing but a pawn for the angel of death to toy with, and worst of all, I found pleasure in some parts of it.

He took me back to his chambers, a series of rooms dedicated to the king, where he fed me with food and wine. I accepted, eating and drinking in silence, unable to look at him. The rift between us spread as the silence continued. How odd. We'd been so close this morning, but the balance of power had shifted. He knew my intentions, and I wouldn't be able to surprise him again.

DURING THE DAYS THAT PASSED, he pushed me. Not physically, but mentally. He kept me locked in his rooms, leaving me books to read—which I devoured—and plenty of rich foods and lavish drinks. The balcony that overlooked the waters was also locked, and each time I gazed at the waves, I thought of the gates of the underworld opening. However, the days remained peaceful, with no sign of impending gloom and darkness.

When Kedron was gone, I attempted to break the lock and considered using my magic to burn down the walls. I tested it once, but the stone walls would not yield to fire. I was imprisoned in the castle.

Even though Kedron left me alone most of the day, he returned each evening. I wanted to resist his advances, but eventually, he won me over. It was much easier to lose myself in his seduction. Worse was the fact that I craved him. I wanted his lips against me, and to lie skin to skin, and let pleasure take over my mind.

One morning, after breakfast, I paced. Unable to sit down and read. Kedron had been elusive that morning, an aura of excitement humming around him, and I couldn't help but wonder what he was up to. Lady Enyd entered and behind her followed three servants. They carried white silk, yards of lace, strings of diamonds, and roses. My heart sank because although Kedron had informed me the wedding date had changed, I'd hoped there was still more time.

The servants wrapped me in white, set a string of diamonds around my neck, and let my red hair hang long and loose down to my waist. When I stood in front of the looking glass, I only saw a scared young woman instead of a future queen. I wondered if others would see it too. I'd never imagined the day I'd be married, and my visions had all pointed toward a future with Romulus, a dream that had never come to pass.

A sudden numbness came over me as they led me to the hall. Harp music played, a sweet and enchanting sound, yet my heart hammered in my throat. Lords and ladies rose as I entered, a sea of unfamiliar faces staring back at me. I was alone, without friends, unless Adomos stood among the guards. My stomach twisted, and I wished I hadn't eaten that morning. Kedron would not forgive me for losing my breakfast and embarrassing him in front of his guests.

Taking a deep breath, I lifted my chin, forcing myself to stand tall because I had no alternatives. I'd chosen this path and I could only hope that I'd rise strong later, to end Kedron's reign once and for all. I had a new mission, a new goal, and that was to protect Labraid from demons, by controlling them with the red sword.

A numbness came over me as I walked down the aisle and arrived at Kedron's side. He took my hand, and the words of the blood contract were spoken aloud. I stood like a spectator, watching the ceremony take place. When it came time to speak, I answered woodenly and when, at last, it ended, I lifted the quill to sign my name next to his. The truth resonated through me. I was queen, in a way I'd never imagined possible. Did it come with freedom? I thought not because it seemed, like my mother, I was a victim of the kingdom of men. Escape was the only way I'd gain my freedom again.

I closed my eyes as Kedron's fingers brushed my cheek and when he kissed me, it was both bitter and sweet. I responded. How could I not? Despite his evilness, there was still an allure that ignited my basic need for love. Finally, Kedron placed a silver crown on my head. It was beautiful, encrusted with jewels, and heavy. It took me a moment to adjust to its weight, and as I did, the announcement rang out loud and clear.

"I give you King Kedron Abbadon and Queen Evie Mor."

He lifted our joined hands to the applause of the audience but when we stepped off the dais, a trembling shook the ground.

Kedron's eyes glinted as he turned to me. "It has begun."

33

"The demons," I hissed, squeezing his hand. "I thought you were going to shut the gates. I thought you wouldn't let this happen."

"Once the gates are open, they cannot be closed," Kedron countered.

"Is this what you waited for? Me to become your queen so that I wouldn't have a choice?"

"As my queen, you now have the power to control armies. Everything I have is yours and nothing will stand in your way. Come, let us see what has been wrought."

His words stayed with me as he led me away while the surrounding crowd called out in alarm. Kedron's hand was sure and steady, as though he knew what would happen all along. Perhaps he did.

He'd timed this to perfection. The long train of my gown tripped me up, and I stumbled a few times, but he was sure and steady beside me.

We were already high in the castle, and he led me to one of the balconies that overlooked the waters. The clouds were gray and low over the horizon, and the waves were choppy and high. They rolled and slammed against the shore as though the rocks would break beneath them. Even in the warmth of summer, I shivered because a mass of darkness was coming. I'd been in the castle for almost two months, and I'd done nothing to stop him, stop this. Now doom rolled to our doorstep and the only hope I had was the fact that I was now queen, and Kedron Abbadon would allow me to take up the red sword. He had to because who else would stop the tide and save the capital from being decimated by demons?

Salt stung my tongue and my mouth went dry as I leaned over the railings. I clasped my fingers so tightly around the railing, it cut into the soft skin of my palms. I was Evie Mor, Queen of the Kingdom of Men, taking up my right as firstborn, although I was a bastard child. The knowledge roiled in my gut and suddenly I realized who I was, and who I'd been my entire life without knowing it. I was a goddess, child of a god, and gods did not back down when the storm raged and worst came to pass.

Kedron Abbadon had a vendetta against the gods. He wanted to punish them by calling forth their worst enemy, the devil locked in the underworld, but I had a choice. Despite how much it hurt to consider it, the truth blew through me like the fresh winds of awakening. I did not need Kedron's love to thrive, but he'd given me a taste of something I'd never had. I doubted what he called love was healthy, and he'd never verbally confirmed what we had, only showed me with his actions. Now, it was my turn to show him what I believed about his plan.

He hadn't listened to me, only acted in his personal interest, and for that, he would pay. "Will you take me to the treasury?"

"Wait, just a moment longer," he breathed, the edges of excitement making his voice higher.

He leaned out beside me as a cool wind blew. It tossed his black hair around his pointed ears, and I wondered, dark and beautiful as he was, how anyone had ever stood in his way.

A deep roar drew my gaze back to the waters where it appeared the sky met the ocean. Except as I stared, I realized what I looked at was a wall of water, an enormous wave surging toward us. It was big enough to smash into the castle and I stepped back, mouth dry, stunned as a boom of thunder shook the foundations. Heavy clouds overhead turned from white to gray to black in a matter of seconds. Darkness was coming. Seconds later, rain streamed down, soaking through the fine cloth of my wedding dress. It clung to my body, wet and transparent, and I faced Kedron again, anger and fear making my words harsh.

"Is it worth it to you to destroy the capital city because of your vendetta against the gods?"

This time, he took his eyes off the water and reached out to catch the droplets that gathered on my chin. The dark orbs of his eyes were soft with emotion, and I wondered how many decades he'd waited for this day. "It is. And I choose you, Evie Mor, to be my queen because you are like me. You grew up in the woods, surrounded by those who weren't of your own kind, just like I did. You left to see your mother and father, to be reunited, and find out the lies they'd spread, that they were the source of corruption. If they had chosen differently, you could have grown up with them, loved and cherished. Instead, you were forgotten, trained to become the savior of the world while they continued on with their lives, leaving you to be a toy of the gods, to be tortured and punished for crimes you did not commit. I know what Jezebel did to you and what she did to many others. Your story is not so different from my own, and you are not alone. I see you because you are right where you belong."

I pressed a trembling hand to my mouth to keep the sob instead from escaping. This was what I'd searched for with my heart and soul, someone who finally saw me, who understood my struggles, where I'd come from, and where I was going. Why did it have to be the angel of death?

The voice of the storm howled as his words sank into me. Kedron and I were alike in every way except for one. He had years to perfect his plans, and he'd lashed out, killing and fighting back. I, too, had a choice about who I became. I could follow him into darkness and become the goddess of death, or I could make a different choice and rise victorious.

Lifting my hand, I touched his cheek, the wave of knowledge making my fingertips cold. "You made a choice," I said over the roar of the waters. "You decided no more. No more torture, no more being left for dead, cheated and used, forced to comply and obey. You killed them all and rose victorious, and when you did so, you cursed the gods, for they were the ones who turned your life into this madness. They didn't listen or protect you. They didn't shield you from the woes of the world, so you decided to bring war to their doorsteps. To make them as unhappy as your life was. After all, why should they sit above us in celestial glory, ignoring the pain of this world, ignoring those who pray to them?"

"Finally, you understand."

"I do." I agreed, and it was a relief to let the honesty escape my lips. This was what he'd been trying to tell me all along. Damn the gods and take the world from their hands. I'd sealed my fate when I killed Jezebel with the red sword. It was likely the story had spread and then he came for me, ready to complete the beginning of his ultimate plan.

Together, we turned back to the waters while the waves crashed into the shore and a ball of blue light spring up from the waters. A terrible sound filled the air, and it wasn't the roar of the waves, nor the cries of the people in the capital, shouting and screaming in fear of their lives. It came from the waters as a sickening mass of darkness spread toward the shore. The demons were coming.

My breath came short and fast and the cold prickle of fear went down my spine.

Winged beasts rose from the waters, their skin blue, shooting of fire coming out of their mouths. As they neared, I realized the mass that swarmed in the waters came on ships that rode the terrible waves. They were too far away to make out, but it was just like the dream, the vision I'd had, blue devils circling the castle on a cliff. It was coming true, which meant this was where I meant to be.

Kedron took my arm, pulling me back from the brink. His gaze raked down my ruined wedding gown and with a sigh he announced. "It is time."

34

The foundations of the castle shook as we made our way to the treasury, the sounds of chaos chasing us. Hysterical crying, calming whispers, and low whimpers. No one came out to face to king, demanding what was happening, and what he'd do to stop it. They, too, were afraid of him, even though they'd stayed by his side. Perhaps he had done something good for the capital by relieving them of the corruption brought on by the kingdom of men, but it was too late for speculation, too late to discover if he was good after all.

Kedron unlocked the doors and ushered me inside. Within, the musty air closed around us and the stone walls hemmed out the chaos from outside. The silence after the noise left my ears ringing and my eyes flickered toward the red sword. It lay where I'd left it days ago, on the floor. I wondered what would happen if anyone touched it, and whether it would burn them the way it had burned Jezebel.

A low hum filled the room as the sword awoke, its voice whispering in my mind.

"Put these on," Kedron instructed, pointing to a pile of clothes and armor.

Pivoting, I stripped out of my wedding gown, not caring that the fabric tore in places, and pulled on the armor. It was comfortable; the tunic molded to my skin, the mail over it lightweight and not too heavy on my shoulders. I put gauntlets around my legs and arms to block the blow of swords, and as I pulled on boots, the tension of battle pumped through me.

I reached for the helmet, hesitating as I stared at it. I'd never worn one before and the thought of being hemmed into steel while others fought made my breath come fast. Ironic, how it was the idea of closing my face inside a helmet that brought a fresh bloom of fear, instead of the fact that I was going out to fight demons.

"At least wear the crown," Kedron's gentle voice came.

I lifted my gaze to his, taking in the diamond

circlet he held out. He placed it on my head, tucking strands of hair into it.

"This signifies your status as queen. As you are officially. My armies are now yours to command and with the red sword, the demons are yours to control. Ours to control."

"Ours?" I asked, my breath ebbing away as a fresh fear seized me. I knew there had to be a reason he waited for the day of our wedding because he'd planned this, timed it to perfection, and yet I was still surprised. Ducking my head, I wove my hair into a braid and tossed it behind my back, waiting for him to respond.

"Aye. Ours," he confirmed. "The red sword was forged here, and the one who carries it controls the fate of the underworld, yet you do not fully understand, do you? The red sword belongs to the rulers of the kingdom of men unless gifted to someone else. Our union means that you and I both have control over the blade. We can both summon it, control its voice, and use it in a time of need."

Unable to keep the shock from my face, I slipped to the floor, my knees too weak to hold me up. A rush of pain went through my side as though I'd been stabbed, but I knew it was only the rush of disappointment and the sick sensation of what I had to do.

The red sword lay an arm's length away. I picked it up, holding the hilt in one hand and the flat side of the blade in the other. Standing, I held it up, as though I would present it to Kedron Abbadon. He had tricked and blindsided me, and the worst part about it was that I fully understood why he did what he did. His story was my story with only one minor difference, a choice. To choose light instead of darkness, hope instead of pain. I refused to give in to the anger, fury, and darkness that threatened to rise and spiral into a whirlwind of violence.

Tears streamed down my face as I approached him, a lump swelling so thick in my throat, the words hurt to say. "Kedron Abbadon. Angel of death. I see you. I could have loved you, but this, this is too much."

And then I moved faster than I'd ever moved before. Squeezing my fingers around the hilt, I drove the sword into his heart.

At first, he didn't react, but slowly his expression changed to one of stunned surprise. His eyes went wide and his head dropped forward, staring at the sword in his heart. Slowly he sank to his knees, blood filling his mouth as he met my gaze, and within it wasn't horror or pity but deep despairing sadness.

A whisper of gurgling words came out of his

mouth. "It was always you, wasn't it? My salvation and my demise."

I nodded through my tears as he fell back, staring until his eyes glazed over in death. I pulled the sword from his body, which seemed so small without his life and spirit inside. Sinking to my knees beside him, I wept great big wrecking sobs that threatened to break me in half.

When at last the tears gave out, a hollowness filled me. I blew my nose on a dry spot of my ruined wedding dress and rose to my feet. Suddenly, nineteen years of age seemed old for what I had been through. I'd even been married for a few scant hours, and now I was the queen of the kingdom of men. Even that realization did not stir up any emotions as I cleaned off the red sword.

Oddly enough, its voice in my head was quiet, and it hadn't burned Kedron's body. I almost wished it had. Anything to take away the emptiness inside. Was it because he was one of its masters? I'd never know.

Pushing open the heavy doors, I walked out into the sacred hall and my eyes widened in alarm. Standing shoulder to shoulder, row to row, were warriors clad in black, helms raised as they waited. They filled the hall, as far as the eye could see, and my jaw worked as I gaped in astonishment.

One by one, they clasped their hands to their hearts and saluted. "All Hail the Queen!"

The thunder of their words roared into me and my heart skipped a beat as I struggled to catch my breath. One by one, the clatter of steel sounded as they kneeled, one knee on the ground, fist planted on the knee and head bowed.

By making me queen, Kedron had not only given me the kingdom but his army of warriors. And I carried the red sword. I lifted my chin and the hollowness inside faded, replaced with determination. All was not lost. The kingdom no longer lay under the spell of Kedron's seductiveness. I would save it, once and for all. The swirl of magic bloomed within, and I lifted my hand palm up. A red flame sprouted from my fingers.

Lifting the red sword, I held it high, and while no words of wisdom or strength or encouragement came to my lips, my voice did not waver when I spoke. "Today, we fight against the demons. Kill them all!"

My army roared in response. As one, they rose, drew their weapons, and marched away. The sound of their stomping echoed through the hall, shedding all semblance of sacredness.

Ideally, I should be the one to lead them as their queen, but I didn't know which way to go to secure the castle or reach the rocky shore where the demons might come ashore. A sense of urgency raced through me until I noticed one warrior who had not joined the others.

Stepping forward, he took off his helmet, casting it aside as he approached me.

Blue skin. Golden eyes. Runes that shone like the sun. My emotions threatened to wreck me again, but I squeezed the sword as Adomos paused in front of me. "Are you well, little one?"

I nodded once.

"It is finished?"

"Aye." I breathed. "It is done."

35

An ominous fog covered the sky, spreading like seeds in a windstorm. By the time Adomos and I reached the shore, my army was already there, waiting. A squall over the waters roared, and out of the fog sailed ships, much larger now that I was on the beach. My heart skipped a beat as creatures materialized from those ships, splashing over the sides in water that came up to their chests. Drums beat in a distance, a hollow thud, but which army the drums belonged to, I could not tell.

The blast of a horn made me jump, and I jerked my head up. The towers of the castles were already hidden in fog, but the call came from one of them, a battle horn. A call to arms or a signal to flee the city.

It served as a reminder that the first battle for Labraid would take place right here on the shores. If the armies of Kedron Abbadon—no, my armies—could not hold the demons at bay, they would swarm the land. We had to hold the city, we could not fail. I could not fail again.

My grip on the red sword tightened, and then I sheathed it. I knew it was the weapon I was supposed to use to control the demons, the sword of a slayer, but perhaps there was another way. I'd use it as a last resort, but I sensed that when the ships reached the shore, the greater demons would not relent. Squinting, I could make out their shapes and forms. They were much bigger than humans, taller, I guessed, than even Adomos.

Bracing myself for impact, I raised my hands and reached deep down into my well of magic. Summoning my strength, fire, and determination, I let it build. Raindrops stung my upturned face, burning as though what fell from the sky was poisoned. I continued to pull, gathering a storm of magic, my lips moving. Kedron Abbadon was right. Despite his words, I still had a deep faith in the gods. I believed they always heard my cries, even when I felt alone. Surely, this time, they would take action and come to my aid.

I opened my palms to receive before aiming at

the waves. Bolts of fire roared out of my hands, twisting as the inferno poured into the ocean. Waves slapped up, rising to meet the fire and quash it, but it continued to burn. One ship caught fire and demonic shrieks filled the air as creatures leaped over the sides, fleeing the burning vessel.

"Move to higher ground," Adomos shouted.

I stepped back as a wave curled, as though the demons controlled the waters too. Adomos grabbed me just in time, tossing me to a higher rock as waves pounded the coastline. Below, the army went down, bowed over in the water, and out there, the demons advanced.

Water and fire did not mix, I already knew that. The ship I'd set fire to had already gone out, a floating char in the waters. Still, I funneled my flames into another inferno, hoping the heat pouring off me in waves would be hot enough to evaporate the moisture and burn the demon. As the waters receded, they came ashore and my army roared, creating a shield wall as they recovered from the waters. Standing shoulder to shoulder, they put their feet together, leaned forward, and pushed against the onslaught.

I targeted another ship as my army pushed the demons back, and a thrill rose within me. Ship after ship caught fire, mutilated creatures leaped over the sides, howling as they fought through the churn toward the shores. A whistling sound filled the air, and I jerked my head back, realizing that archers were along the rocks high above me. A volley of arrows loosened, picking off the demons in the water, targeting the ships I hadn't burned yet. We'd drive them back if we kept fighting like this, and I wondered if this had been Kedron Abbadon's plan and who controlled the army. Had they been instructed, earlier, on warfare and what to do? Because it was clear the foot soldiers in the water knew how to fight the demons, and the archers needed no guidance in picking off the easy targets trying to climb the shore.

I lost track of time as we fought. The archers thinning the lines of demons; the army holding them at bay on the shore while I burned the ships. It wasn't easy, but the path to victory was clear. At least that was what I assumed when a terrible thunder shook the ground itself. I lost my balance and fell, scraping my palms against a sharp rock. Out in the oceans, an impossible wave rose, and a sickening sensation swirled in my belly. Something was coming, and slowly my knowledge about the world pieced together.

Demons had plagued Labraid for a long time, sneaking out of the cracks where the barrier that kept them in the underworld was weak. They were the lesser demons, while the greater ones weren't exactly demons. They were Nephilim, like Adomos and even Kedron Abbadon, a blend of the world below and the world above. But what came out of the depths of the ocean, using the gates which had been opened, were monsters. These were the greater demons and even from a distance, I saw them riding the waves. Tentacles, slobbering fangs, and darkness that made my heart grow cold.

The fog rolled deeper, blinding the stars, hiding the celestial lights from the fate of Labraid and the horror which was to come. I had to do something, but a numbness consumed me. Fear wormed its way into my heart and I froze, unable to react as a tidal wave slammed into the shore.

It hurt. I hadn't known how badly water could sting when it rolled like a wave. It flung me against the rocks and I had the presence of mind not to scream. Instead, I thrust my hands out, my magic just enough to create a shield that hovered over my face, protecting it from the worst of the onslaught. My body took the brunt of it, waves slamming against my torso, my feet knocked into a crevice between rocks, twisting as the water poured over them. Squeezing my eyes shut, I willed the pain away and waited for the wave to relent.

Beyond me came screamed and cries, roars of pain and suffering. I heard snapping, as though something was breaking. Thunder rumbled, rained poured down, and wind slammed against me. It was cold, oh so cold, and my teeth chattered as I forced my eyes to open and my shield faded. Seaweed covered the rocks, and some of it had slashed open my exposed skin.

I coughed, tasting blood, and struggled to sit up. The armor had done its job of protecting me from the worst of the storm, but my body still ached from being thrown as though I weighed nothing. All thoughts of winning faded as I craned back my head and stared up, up, up, at the abomination rising from the waters.

36

My mouth gaped open, and suddenly I understood while Kedron Abbadon had looked forward to this day. The beginning of his war against the gods. The first waves of creatures had been nothing. Demons, yes, but they were nothing compared to the beast that rose out of the ocean, red scales glistening like lava. What I at first assumed were tentacles were seven heads with white horns and a crown on each one. Those heads roared and bellowed and fire shot from its mouth. Around it, ships were tossed by the wayside and suddenly I realized the demons that had come ahead weren't coming to take over the land. They were desperate to escape the beast.

I spun, but there was nowhere to flee as the

seven-headed red dragon moved for the shore. My limbs trembled as I stood tall, and when I lifted my hands to use magic, the well within me was empty. Hollowed out by the blasts of infernos I'd send during the first wave. Below me, my army moved on the shore, looking like tiny ants as they scrambled to reform the line and raise their shields.

This was what we were up against, and magic was the only way to keep the capital city from falling. Except as I lifted my arms, I knew it would take a powerful act, something much greater than magic, to keep the red dragon at bay. It would take the combined power of the gods and nature to move against it. My fingers twitched as they closed around the hilt of the sword.

It rang out as I drew it, and a voice whispered to my ears, different from before. Within was still the lust for violence and death, but this time I understood it, like a key unlocking the truth, much as I'd understood Kedron Abbadon in those final moments. The sword wanted to destroy because it echoed the heart of a demon. After being bound in darkness and lasting torment, all the goodness had been burned away into one frightening desire for vengeance. But I did not know how I could control it, how to keep the darkness from suffocating the light within me.

As I stood, warring with my conscience, the seven-headed dragon roared, sending gushers of fire across the waters. The heat of it was so intense, my skin went hot and salt stung my eyes. This was war. Against a monster that did not belong in this world. The water caught fire as the dragon advanced and demons swarmed around it. The wind whipped up and rain poured down so hard that between it and the fog, it was difficult to see what was in front of my face, but I could not miss the glitter of crimson scales and the body of the dragon, larger than the castle as it neared.

Below me on the shore, the demons drove through the army, shattering shields, cleaving limbs from bodies in their desperation to reach the cliffs. A few had already started clambering onto the rocks, and the part of the army chased them. Arrows whistled, striking at random. One hurled out of the fog so close to my cheek it almost grazed my skin. This was madness. I sensed the panic in the air, the not knowing what to focus on, who to fight, and worst of all was the fear.

The storm made the air oppressive, and with the wind and rain, it was difficult to tell friend from foe. Shapes blurred around me, and the helms with the signature of Kedron Abbadon were impossible to see. Now was the time for me to act, and yet a sense of confusion plagued me. I needed to face the dragon and take it down, but if I did, I'd surely die.

Deep down inside, I knew I was alone. No one would tell me what to do, or how to kill the monster from the deep. Part of me wondered if I'd waited to kill Kedron Abbadon until after the war if he could have stood against the dragon. But no, he would have taken advantage of my indecision and used the red sword. I could not let the world slip away from my hands. Action, not indecision, had to guide me.

The fear of battle of blood raged around me and I closed my eyes, focused on the sword, and let everything sink away. Even though I hadn't read the scrolls, and knew even less about where the sword was forged and how to control it, I had a deep well of magic. I was powerful. Kedron had told me about my father, how he waged war against the supernatural. He might not be here now, but I hoped he'd given me his strength and spirit. To wage this war right here and now and win.

Originally, I assumed killing Kedron Abbadon would be enough, and I refused to think about what he meant to me. It wasn't enough, only the start of a new era, which would be ushered in. Even if, by some miracle, the army could overwhelm the demons and drive them back, some would still escape and lose themselves in the world to cause chaos. Not to mention the seven-headed dragon. It bellowed, bathing the rocks with fire.

Coughing, I threw my arms up, trying to create a shield of magic to block my face from the chipped stones and burning ash that smote the air. Beyond the fog, it was impossible to see anything other than the dragon, which neared, and my concentration was ruined. Planting my feet again on the shaking stones, I tried again to concentrate, but when I closed my eyes, Kedron's voice echoed in my mind. I had to control the sword instead of letting it control me, and it was possible because I was a goddess.

I recalled my training in Anon Loam, and my kind instructor, Donia, explaining about magic and how it worked. When it had quickened within in me I was surprised because I'd always had magic, even though I considered it useless. When I was young, it appeared as flares of colors, because I had no control over it. But once I tapped into it and learned how to use it, it became as easy as breathing. Perhaps the red sword was the same way. I kept trying to figure it out, control it while suppressing the voice that rang out loud and clear. Kill. Kill. Kill.

It was there, resounding in the depths of my being, but this time, instead of fighting it, I opened up my spirit and welcomed the voice. It surged through me, the lust for violence and death, for warfare and blood, and most importantly, to need to destroy every living being that stood in its way, demon or not. I let it come. I welcomed the darkness, and as it filled me, something else happened. The key to controlling the sword unlocked, just as my magic had in Anon Loam.

There. Something twisted inside of me and then broke. I squeezed the sword as a flash of jagged red lightning split the sky. It came from the sword; it came from me. Blinding red light flared around me as I opened my eyes, cutting through the fog like a blade. Holding one hand out, I lifted the sword and ran, even though the ground shook. Even though I lost my footing. What was inside of me was more than enough. I leaped off a rock and dove toward the waters and the seven-headed dragon.

37

Once I opened my spirit to the sword, sensations passed through me in a blur. I had the vision of an eagle, seeing better than I had before, even through the fog. The sword cleaved demons open, creating a path to the waters where the monster lurked. My army was in disarray, some fighting, others fleeing. Arrows hitting both friendly and unfriendly targets. Bodies were on fire, and even the flood of waters could not stop the destruction. The foundations of the rock trembled, and the water and fire had eroded the original shoreline. Crevices had opened up underneath the castle and demons scaled the cliffs, eager to reach the top and invade the city.

Above me flew a flock of blue harpies, screeching

into the wind, the storm making their howls more frantic. In a blur, they were gone, and I could only imagine what must be happening in the city. Had anyone called to evacuate it, or shield the people who lived there against what was coming? Or had this been Kedron's plan all along? To cause destruction no one would forget. Delegates from across Labraid had come for the wedding ceremony, and if they hadn't fled already, they were likely caught in the crosshairs of the battle. And if they died, who would take their place and lead their people?

This was what he meant, a cleansing that would rock the foundations of Labraid, and force a new era to rise. Whether or not I liked what he'd done, I was part of it, and it was my magic that would determine whether good or evil reigned.

With my spirit open, the babbling of the demons echoed in my ears. They were gleeful to have escaped their eternal prison and determined to make the world their own. Wherever they went, they planned on killing the humans and turning Labraid into their paradise. That could not happen.

Their voices buzzed in my mind. Deep and layered, they spoke of death and filth and violence, immediately making me wish I could shut them out of my mind. My limbs trembled, and I squeezed the hilt of the blade so hard it would leave indentions on my palm. The demons were out for vengeance and they were coming for the inhabitants of Labraid like a thief in the night to kill, steal, and destroy. The red sword sang in my mind with the same song: *Kill. Kill. Kill.* Except this time, I knew the sword of the slayer wanted me to pay the ultimate price and kill demons. But how to control them?

I searched my mind for the thread of voices and followed it to a hive of hums. A command raced through my mind, the words an endless chat. One I needed the demons to believe if I would have a chance at all. *This world does not belong to you. Seek the darkest places in the world. Run. Hide. I am coming for you. This world does not belong to you. Seek the darkest places in the world. Run. Hide. I am coming for you.* Over and over, I let the words whisper through my mind, hoping to reach their subconscious with my mind.

Snarling monsters with elongated limbs and claws instead of hands and feet hurled themselves into my path. I cleaved them in half with the sword, and when they fell, their bodies burst into an ooze of black liquid, ash, and one burst into bats which fluttered around me, hissing. I leaped over the prone bodies which would no longer draw breath, a blend of both demons and my army lay in the shallows, the rising water covering their bodies. Ignoring the horror of death, I ran, banishing the vision from my mind.

The only voice that I didn't hear clearly was that of the dragon. By now it had reached the shore, its great lumbering body moving slower than I'd expected. The massive scaled body towered above me, so high it almost reached the castle. Indeed, it reared back and belched fire at the towers, which caught fire. Screams of agony filled the air and without looking, I knew the archers had fallen, the castle that had stood so firmly would fall.

Pushing off a rock, I splashed into the water, the shock of it taking my breath away. The first day I'd come out of the rocks with Kedron, the water had been cool. Now it blazed, steam pouring off it, heating my armor. With a cry of rage, I shoved off the bed of the ocean and leaped. My feet struck red scales, and I climbed, my hands burning as I pulled myself up on the beast's body.

At first, the dragon didn't notice until one head turned and slitted yellow eyes glared at me. A forked tongue twisted out and its fanged mouth opened. It lunged to bite me but the red sword sang, driving up into the roof it is mouth. Salvia dripped down, stinging as it scorched my skin, but I was past emotion, past crying out against the pain. I pulled the sword free, my fury rising, exploding out of me as I drove the sword into the flesh of its neck. The beast howled, and I felt the red sword licking up the bone and blood, melting the flesh while the beast was still alive.

Six heads whipped around, but I kept my hands firmly on the red sword while a strange light glimmered around me. Somehow, someway, my magical shield was working. Fire erupted out of the dragon's mouth and consumed me, but although it swallowed me, I did not feel heat, wind, or rain. The dragon spread its wings and lifted into the air, crying out as it rose. Its body was heavy and slow to move, but on its back, the castle tilted, the waters shifted below me and thunder boomed.

As a flash of lightning lit up the sky, sparks of light drew my attention. My eyes widened as winged creatures holding flaming swords dropped out of the heavens, headed for the battlefield below. Somehow, someway, the gods and goddesses of Labraid had heard my cry for help, and they had come to wage war against the demons.

The fury of my magic faded, and for the first time, I actually held a deep knowledge within that I wasn't alone, unloved, or unwanted. I had a purpose, a unique destiny and while my road was tough at times, help would come when I needed it the most. Indeed, the voice of the sword did not overwhelm me, and the fires that blazed could not touch me. I was a goddess of fire, of myth, of magic, and nothing would stand in my way.

I drew the sword out of the dragon's neck as it bellowed again, and the red magic within me flared brighter and hotter. Lifting the sword, I drove it deep, cleaving through scales and skin, and flesh and bone. The wind roared in circles as the dragon bellowed, wings outstretched over the city. The voice of the red sword sounded and everything exploded.

The blast hurled me outward. Somehow, I held on to the sword as I dropped from the dragon's back. Its severed heads flew in six different directions and its body rained down in jagged chunks, smashing into the city. I spread my arms out, even though I didn't have wings, and the waters rushed up to greet me. Closing my eyes, I called out instructions to the demons who continued to pour out of the waves.

This world does not belong to you. Seek the darkest places in the world. Run. Hide. I am coming for you.

Blinding pain roared around me as I smacked into the waters, and then darkness took me and I knew nothing more.

38

My first awareness after killing the beast was pain. Every inch of my body hurt. Dull throbs in some places, pulsing pain in others. I gritted my teeth, letting a moan escape, but it only increased. White-hot flares danced around me and something solid was pressed to my lips. "Drink. Heal." I managed a few swallows before I sank away into blessed darkness.

The next time I woke, my vision blurred, then cleared as a familiar face hovered above mine. Moli, the castle healer. So, some had survived the chaos. She beamed at me. "It's good to see you awake, my queen. There are many who've been waiting for you to revive. No." She held up a hand. "Don't speak. Your body is still healing. It was quite the fall you took, and I believe you burned yourself from the inside out. Drink more of this. You'll be allowed to have visitors soon."

I drank, wondering at her words, and only catching a glimpse of my body wrapped in bandages. I stayed awake a little longer before passing out again, and when I came to for the third time, Takari's dark eyes met mine.

A slow smile crept to my face, and even though my skin stretching over my cheeks hurt, it was good to have a reason to smile. Wiggling my fingers, I lifted my hand halfway off the bed. "Hello old friend," I croaked. My voice was thick from disuse.

Takari smiled back, and then a sob broke as she pressed her hands against her mouth. She rocked back and forth for a moment, regaining her composure and then. "Oh, Evie. It is good to see you awake again."

"How are you here? Or perhaps, how am I here?" I asked, my voice sinking into a whisper. Anything louder would hurt my throat.

Takari wiped her eyes. "Evie, there's much to tell you. I don't know where to begin, and I don't want to upset you with all that has happened since. . ."

"After all I've been through, I doubt anything you say will upset me."

"Evie." Takari reached out as if to take my hand

and then pulled back. "I can't imagine what you've been through."

I turned my head away, blinking as memories rose, poignant and oh so real. I could still taste his lips and smell mint on my skin, and worst of all, see the slack surprise on his face when I plunged the sword into his heart. Suddenly, any news was better than sitting here, letting my memories replay in my mind over and over again. I did what needed to be done, but it would take a long time to heal physically, mentally, and emotionally. "Don't spare me anything, just talk."

A flood of words poured off her tongue. "I always thought it was odd how you never returned after leaving to regain the supplies. But then the supplies were delivered by none other than the faerie, and I knew something was wrong. I wrote the note, hoping it would reach your hands, and I begged Nolani to do something. In the weeks that passed, the woods were oddly quiet until one day the scouts reported that a blue shadow haunted the wood. I hoped it might be Adomos, and I took a chance to go out with the riders. I snuck away when I could because I knew if Adomos had come, you might be with him. We met, and he told me about your plan, and how help was needed. It was a terrible time, trying to convince the council we needed to at least send scouts to the capital to confirm with what Adomos said was true, and then, oh Evie, we heard about the wedding."

I turned away, hating to see the pity in her eyes. "It was my choice. I don't need you to feel sorry for me."

"Still, I can't imagine what that must have been like."

Tears made it impossible to speak for a moment, and I struggled with words. It was hard to breathe for a few moments. I was well aware it was a grief I'd carry with me for a long time. "Please, go on, tell me what happened after Adomos came. I want to know everything."

Takari sighed. "The defenders have long been awaiting the death of Kedron Abbadon, and the day when the capital city would be free to be regained again. They gathered warriors, stationed in nearby cities, hiding in the woods, and prepared to take action when the time came. Scouts went into the city. I must admit, the defenders did not trust Adomos to provide accurate news. On the day of the wedding, reports came back that there was a disturbance in the waters, and then all hell broke. I was traveling toward the capital when all this happened, and the demons broke into the world. We'd already gathered arms and defenders had warned the elves who had their own scouts in the capital. But no one was prepared for what came out of the water, and I only heard reports of the monster you slayed with the red sword. I was wrong about it, Evie. I always thought it would destroy you. I guess I listened to the old tales, and I never believed anyone, not even a goddess, could control the legendary sword."

"What happened after?" I asked breathlessly. "To the demons and the city? Are we in the castle?"

Takari shook her head, expression wary. "No, the castle fell into the ocean, and the city is in ruins. Many demons escaped, running into the wilds and while the land is ripe with fear, there is also hope because of what you did. The stories about you are already spreading, and I'm afraid everyone knows who you are now. They call you Evie Mor, Goddess of Myth and Magic, Demon Slayer. There are whispers too, that you're the last queen of the kingdom of men because of your marriage."

"So I'm back in the Hall of Defenders?" I confirmed. "And what about my siblings?"

Takari nodded. "They are here too. It took a week to transport you back, and we took in as many refugees from the city as possible, including the castle healer Moli. She said you'd welcome her company. It's been a month since the battle, and even now raiding parties are going out, scouring the countryside for demons, hunting and killing those they find. Labraid is different now. Many royals died when the capital city fell, and many peoples and tribes are searching for new leadership. A new era is coming to Labraid, and we get to determine what kind of world we live in. Instead of being victims of it, we can shape it."

A tear leaked out of my eye and dripped down my chin. We, the new generation, would shape the land of Labraid. It was a fresh start, just as Kedron Abbadon had wanted, although not exactly the way he had in mind. He'd been so patient with his plan until the very end, but what was done was done, and I had to focus on healing instead of rewinding pieces of the past.

"Brianna asked to speak with you when you are ready."

I didn't know if I had the strength for her attitude. Even so, I nodded. "Send her in."

I rested my eyes while I waited, and soon a light step came and Brianna's frame filled the doorway. She leaned on it a moment, looking at me before entering. Her hair was down, flowing about her shoulders, and a new light graced her face. Hope.

"I came to say thank you," she said, all in a rush. "I didn't know what extremes you'd use to free us, and I'd hoped the city might stand so that I could be queen. But I think what you did was right. The kingdom of men was corrupt, and it is no more. None shall rule that cursed city again."

"You're free. What will you do?"

Brianna shrugged, although a smile played around her lips. "I always thought I'd rule, but perhaps one's kingdom is one's home. I'd like some land, a house, a garden, and to come and go as I please. The defenders are searching for a place somewhere out there, and Evie, you're always welcome, although I doubt you'll settle anywhere. You have fire in you veins and a warrior's heart. I'm sure the mundane will be too dull for you."

Dull. "I could use a bit of dullness, especially after what happened at the capital."

Brianna nodded. "You look much better than you did when they first brought you here. All your skin was gone and your veins were showing. Moli the healer worked a miracle, so it would seem, but everyone is singing your praises. And everyone knows you're a goddess." Even softer, she added. "And the last queen of men. I think Mother wanted everything that had been stolen to be returned to us, and the kingdom retaken. But after Father—my father, the king—found out the truth, he left, and the trolls killed him. Mother never forgave herself, and it made her even more determined to win, to gain something after everything had been taken away. But I believe this is better. The pressure of ruling is gone, and Labraid will become full of free people who will rule themselves."

I gave her a wry look, which she returned with one of her own, then backed toward the door. "Heal well, older sister. I'm sure I'll talk to you soon."

It was only when she left that I realized she'd called me sister, and a wistfulness filled my heart because I knew my journey wasn't over yet. I had more to do, and at last, I wanted to travel to Dun'gilly and visit my father.

39

On the eve of my twentieth birthday, I climbed a hillock in the wildlands, weaving through a fragrant green forest on my way to meet with a god, more specifically, my father, Dagda. A sharp wind whistled, sending the dead leaves from fall swirling in tiny circles. The shrill hoots of the Amaca birds filled the air as they searched for the ideal tree branch for a nest. The air was ripe with the promise of spring, and warmth filled my heart. After months of healing, I'd finally set off for the hills of Dun'gilly, and now I was mere moments away.

"There it is, just beyond those trees," Adomos said, pulling back a branch to create an opening in the foliage.

Adomos. It had taken some time to find him again, but the words he'd sworn to me were true. Takari, always protective of me, was mistrustful of what he'd allowed me to do. But that was what I liked about Adomos. He treated me like an equal, and besides, he'd sworn to serve me. Despite everything that had happened, or because of it, he understood me the most, and he did not judge me.

Standing on my tiptoes, I peered through the foliage. Beyond the greenery rose a gray mountain, a crater of rubble and rock surrounding it. Rivers of lava flowed from the side and pooled around it, an effective barrier to keep everyone away. The mountain was an eyesore amid a lush valley and difficult to believe my father, the god Dagda, lived there.

"Dun'gilly Mountain," I whispered, and clenched my fists. My body went tense as I stared, recalling the moment I met my birth mother and the swift disappointment that followed. This time, though, I was prepared. I'd go meet my father, with no expectations, only questions, and then I'd leave. Adomos and I had our quest, and I still carried the red sword because across Labraid demons lay in hiding. It was my mission to seek them out and destroy them. After all, I carried the sword of a slayer, and I knew who I was, a protector of Labraid.

"We won't reach it until nightfall," Adomos said.

His deep voice jerked me out of my thoughts. “Are you suggesting we make camp now?”

“Let’s get closer until we reach the end of the wood, and Evie, the wood is as far as I go. You know that I cannot get close to the gods.”

I nodded, aware that in the end, I’d go on alone. “Aye, one more night in the woods,” I agreed, rubbing my hands together.

The calls of the birds died away, and I chewed my lower lip. An additional worry broke through my thoughts. What if my father wasn’t welcoming? All this time I’d based my need to see him on the fact that he owed me. I was his forsaken daughter. The least he could do was give me answers. But gods and goddesses were treacherous, and he might be like Jezebel, selfish and cruel. Turning a blind eye to anything but his needs.

“You are anxious,” Adomos noted.

A plume of red magic danced on my fingertips. Tucking my hands under my arms, I banished it. “I’m preparing myself. I don’t expect him to be as welcoming as my mother. In fact, I don’t know what to expect.”

“It is natural to have doubts when faced with the apex of change. You’ve been strong, but you’re also searching for the truth and this moment is important for you. You will go in, hold your head up high, and take what you need. Don't let his words sway you from who you are."

I cocked my head, gazing up at him. "True, I know who I am. I'm tempted to walk away without meeting him, but if I don't go now, I'll always wonder."

Adomos's heavy hand landed on my shoulder, spinning me to face him. An awareness of his height and breadth made my face flush. "You should go and ask, even though you know who you are. Lest you forget, you are Evie Mor, Goddess of Myth and Magic, Demon Slayer, Last Queen of the Kingdom of Men. You don't answer to anyone, but meeting your father is a turning point for you. Despite what he says or does, you are whoever you declare yourself to be, and nothing anyone says or does can change that. You have great magic and control, you've already done much in your young years, and meeting your father does not define you. All the same, I hope it provides you with the clarity you've been seeking."

Placing my hand on his wrist, I stared up at him. "You're right, but you always are. Thank you, Adomos."

He gave me a slight smile, and we stayed that way for a moment, looking at each other as the wind blew stronger, a reminder we were in a sacred place.

We made camp that evening under the shadow of the mountain, and the stars of eld came out to grace us with their splendor. They reminded me of the peaceful time Adomos and I spent together by the lake, and how the world had paused, giving us a moment to prepare. Everything had changed since then and even more after the battle in the capital city. I slept deeply that night and my sleep was dreamless.

IN THE MORNING I walked up the mountain, sidestepping the pools of lava. It was warm, but not the intense heat I expected from a volcano. I'd left Adomos waiting for me under the shady boughs, and now that I was alone, my emotions warred with me.

What if Dagda wasn't home? What if he wouldn't give me answers? But I held onto the control of my magic and forced my mind to drift away, back to the Meditation Meadow where everything was peaceful, controlled, and only my intentions set things in motion.

As I focused my mind, my anxiety faded, and a door appeared. Eying the door skeptically, I paused in front of it. I was only halfway up the mountainside, and below me, a river of lava flowed into stones. This was ash and dust—devastation. The home of a god should not be like this. I'd envisioned Dun'gilly to be more like Elsdore, which was called the hills of the gods because of its beauty. This wasn't, and a warning stirred within as I placed my palm against the door.

It lit up with crimson words. I only caught snatches of them before the door gave a shudder and opened. Light streamed out, and I walked through, my jaw dropping as I understood. The dusty volcano was all an illusion to deter trespassers, and I walked into the real mountain.

A forest of giant pines and the scent of birch filled the air. Lifting my head, I breathed deeply, inhaling the lavender flowers and tasting the purity in the air. Bright yellow buds lined the path. Bluebirds fluttered overhead, and a white-tailed deer peeked out from behind a tree before continuing to graze.

A flash of silver drew my attention as a pack of wolves trotted past, no doubt hunting the deer. Birds called to each other, but what made me cock my head was the low undercurrent of music which hummed through the land. Suddenly my weight would no longer hold me, and I kneeled. I stood on sacred land.

Pressing my hands into the dirt, I breathed in the scent of life and it felt so familiar. From the ground, we came, formed from ash and dust, birthed into a new creation of life. Upon our deaths, we'd return to the ground and the cycle would continue. But here, as I pressed my hands against the earth, reminded of the vision the gods had given me in the Beluar Woods, I knew with certainty that I had come home. At last.

I remained on the ground a long time, listening, breathing, while tears wet my face. This was where I belonged. This was the source where magic and power filled me with determination and strength. All along I'd questioned myself and my quest, but here there were no worries, no questions, only peace.

I didn't hear the footfalls nor sense the shadow that passed over me. It wasn't until a deep voice rumbled above me that I realized I wasn't alone.

"You must be her."

Lifting my head, I took in a man, nay, a god. He stood planted like a tree, hands on his hips, flaming red hair springing from his head like a bush. A thick beard reached his broad chest. He was stout, jolly, and fearsome, with a giant ax on his back. Emerald green eyes lit up as he grinned at me and opened up his arms.

I stood, and suddenly it all became clear—my path, who I was, and all the trials and tribulations I'd gone through. It was the cycle of growth, forming me, molding me into a goddess. Looking back, all the hard times and struggles were necessary because, without them, I wouldn't be here, and I wouldn't have had the determination to do what I had done.

Confidence buoyed me forward, and I walked into his arms. "Hello, Father."

Thank you for reading *Goddess of Myth and Magic.*

I hope you enjoyed this tale and the completion of Evie's adventures, and would be honored if you'd leave a review.

Leave a Review on Amazon

Visit my shop for more: https://angelajford.com/collections/gods-and-goddesses-of-labraid

EXCLUSIVE SHORT STORY

Don't miss this exclusive short story.

He's an immortal fae knight, she's a cursed warrior. To save their people from annihilation, they must go where the living have never gone before.

Every few years, the swarm comes, a terrifying pestilence that consumes the living. One sting from the deadly creatures brings not death but something much worse. . .

Every few years, Rainer, a fae knight sworn to protect the mountains, prepares his people to lose everything.

No one knows why the swarm comes, and no one can stop it.

Except for her.

Zelma is a warrior, sent to find the legendary firedrakes

in the mountain. Instead, she's attacked by the swarm and left to die.

When she awakens in the hall of the fae knight, she's determined to continue her quest.

However, the sting has changed her, and new, frightening abilities awaken.

Afraid of becoming the target of the fae knight's wrath, she fights to control her magic as they travel into the heart of the mountains.

Will Rainer and Zelma save their people? Or will her magic kill them first?

Of Fae and Flame **is a complete, stand-alone short story set in the Nomadian universe.**

Only available at: https://angelajford.com/product/of-fae-and-flames/

ALSO BY ANGELA J. FORD

Join my email list for updates, previews, giveaways, and new release notifications. Join now: www.angelajford.com/signup

The Four Worlds Series (epic fantasy)

A complete four-book epic fantasy series spanning two hundred years, featuring an epic battle between mortals and immortals.

Legend of the Nameless One Series (epic fantasy)

A complete five-book epic fantasy adventure series featuring an enchantress, a wizard, and a sarcastic dragon.

Night of the Dark Fae Trilogy (romantic epic fantasy)

A complete epic fantasy trilogy featuring a strong heroine, dark fae, orcs, goblins, dragons, antiheroes, magic, and romance.

Tales of the Enchanted Wildwood (fairy tale romance)

Adult fairy tales blending fantasy action-adventure with steamy romance. Each short story can be read as a stand-alone and features a different couple.

Tower Knights (fantasy romance)

Gothic-inspired adult steamy fantasy romance. Each novel can be read as a stand-alone and features a different couple.

Gods & Goddesses of Labraid (epic fantasy)

A warrior princess with a dire future embarks on a perilous quest to regain her fallen kingdom.

Lore of Nomadia Trilogy (epic fantasy romance)

The story of an alluring nymph, a curious librarian, a renowned

hunter, and a mad sorceress as they seek to save—or destroy—the empire of Nomadia.

Visit angelajford.com for autographed books, exclusive book swag and book boxes.

ABOUT THE AUTHOR

Angela J. Ford is a best-selling author who writes epic fantasy and steamy fantasy romance with vivid worlds, gray characters, and endings you just can't guess. She has written and published over twenty books.

She enjoys traveling, hiking, and playing World of Warcraft with her husband. First and foremost, Angela is a reader and can often be found with her nose in a book.

Aside from writing, she enjoys the challenge of working with marketing technology and builds websites for authors.

If you happen to be in Nashville, you'll most likely find her enjoying a white chocolate mocha and daydreaming about her next book.

facebook.com/angelajfordauthor
twitter.com/aford21
instagram.com/aford21
amazon.com/Angela-J-Ford/e/B0052U9PZO
bookbub.com/authors/angela-j-ford